JOE COLTON'S JOURNAL

There's been a strange vibe in the air ever since I got off the phone with my son Rand. He's on his way home with some shocking news that he has to deliver in person. I wonder what it could be...? Meanwhile, on the home front, Chance Reilly is back in Prosperino. He returned to look in on his terminally ill father, but the old coot died before they had a chance to make amends. After Chance's mother died when he was a lad, he was left to battle his tyrannical, verbally abusive father alone—except for that rebellious teenage year when he stayed at the Hopechest Ranch and Hacienda de Alegria. Now his old man is making Chance's life miserable, even from the grave. His airtight last testament decrees that Chance must be married in order to inherit the family ranch and estate. As luck would have it, his father's private duty nurse, Lana Ramirez, offered to be his temporary wife—on the condition that Chance agree to father her baby! Hmm...could Old Man Reilly have had this ace up his sleeve all along?

About the Author

CARLA CASSIDY

Wealth, power, secrets and dysfunction...the Colton family has it all, and Carla was thrilled to be among the writers who got the opportunity to bring this fascinating family to life.

In *Pregnant in Prosperino,* she not only got the opportunity to explore elements of evil, but also enjoyed breathing life into two wonderful characters who find the goodness and joy of true love.

Carla Cassidy is an award-winning author who lives in the Midwest with her husband, Frank, and their two neurotic dogs.

Pregnant in Prosperino

Carla Cassidy

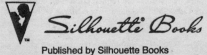

Published by Silhouette Books
America's Publisher of Contemporary Romance

Special thanks and acknowledgment are given to Carla Cassidy for her contribution to THE COLTONS series.

SILHOUETTE BOOKS
300 East 42nd St.,
New York, N. Y. 10017

ISBN 0-373-38714-8

PREGNANT IN PROSPERINO

Visit Silhouette at www.eHarlequin.com

Printed in U.S.A.

THE COLTONS

Meet the Coltons—
a California dynasty with a legacy of privilege and power.

Chance Reilly: *Rancher desperately seeking something.*
A rebellious bad boy in his teens, this rancher now
feels empty and rootless. Could the hasty marriage he
enters into to save his family ranch be his solution?

Lana Ramirez: *Pregnant in Prosperino.* Though she's
carrying his baby, this nurse senses that Chance is a
footloose, rambling man who'll soon move on. But if
she has her way, the only place this cowboy will be
heading is...back into her ever-loving arms!

Joe Colton: *The perplexed patriarch.* When the police
arrive to arrest his wife, Joe is shocked to discover
that his *real* wife, Meredith, was a victim of a malicious
plot. Now that Meredith's impostor twin, Patsy, is
behind bars, this reunited couple has some lost years
to catch up on.

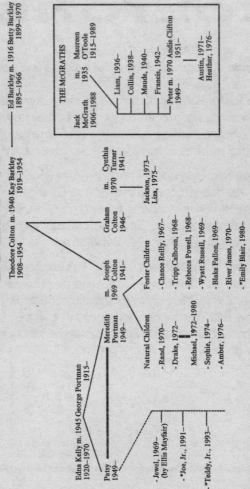

THE COLTONS

Theodore Colton m. 1940 Kay Barkley
1908–1954   1919–1954

Ed Barkley m. 1916 Betty Barkley
1895–1966   1899–1970

Joseph Colton
1941–   m. 1969

Graham Colton
1946–

m. 1970 Cynthia Turner
1941–

Jackson, 1973–
Liza, 1975–

Edna Kelly m. 1945 George Portman
1920–1970   1915–

Meredith Portman
1949–

Patsy
1949–

Natural Children
- Rand, 1970–
- Drake, 1972–
- Michael, 1972–1980
- Sophie, 1974–
- Amber, 1976–

Foster Children
- Chance Reilly, 1967–
- Tripp Calhoun, 1968–
- Rebecca Powell, 1968–
- Wyatt Russell, 1969–
- Blake Fallon, 1969–
- River James, 1970–
- *Emily Blair, 1980–

- Jewel, 1969–
  (by Ellis Mayfair)
- *Joe, Jr., 1991–
- *Teddy, Jr., 1993–

THE McGRATHS

Jack McGrath m. 1935 Maureen O'Toole
1906–1988   1915–1989

Liam, 1936–
Collin, 1938–
Maude, 1940–
Francis, 1942–
Peter m. 1970 Andie Clifton
1949–   1951–

Austin, 1971–
Heather, 1976–

LEGEND
-- Child of Affair
— Twins
* Adopted by Joe Colton

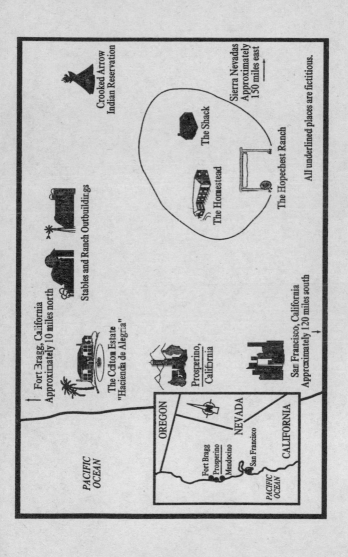

One

"**D**amn you, old man."

Bitterness ripped through Chance Reilly as he stared at his father's fresh grave. In life, Tom Reilly had cheated his son out of a happy childhood and a normal adolescence with his bullying and abuse.

And now, in death, Tom had delivered the final blow to any hope Chance might have had of ever making peace with him, or of inheriting the Reilly ranch.

Chance turned and gazed at the house in the distance. Even the shadows of approaching night couldn't hide the neglect that clung to the place.

The house cried out for a new coat of paint and the weeds were knee-high in places. And that was just the beginning. The barn door hung askew, several railings of the corral were lying on the ground and there was no livestock grazing in the pastures.

Cars lined the drive, letting him know the place was still filled with sympathetic well-wishers and curious neighbors.

He should go back inside and play the role of grieving, dutiful son, but he couldn't just yet. It was difficult to grieve when anger and bitterness were ripping apart your soul.

His gaze left the house and instead focused on his mother's headstone next to his father's final resting place. A lot of help she'd been, dying on him when he'd been eight years old and leaving him alone with ''Sarge,'' as his father had enjoyed being called.

Sarge—who had run his house like an army barrack, who had never been afraid to use hurtful words and flying fists to emphasize a point.

Emotion expanded in Chance's chest and he fought against the suffocating tightness. When he'd gotten the word that his father had taken a turn for the worse, he'd left his motel room in Wichita, Kansas, and had caught the first plane he could get to reach Prosperino, California.

However, his father, perverse to the end, passed away mere hours before Chance had arrived back home, making it impossible for father and son to resolve the acrimony that had marked their relationship for years.

The funeral had been two hours before, and Walter Bishop, the family lawyer, had only a brief time before delivered the last of the bad news to Chance.

''Damn you,'' he said again. ''You were a miserable man who spent your whole life making me miserable.''

''Chance?''

He whirled around at the low, female voice, angry at the intrusion.

He relaxed a bit as he saw Lana Ramirez approach, her long black skirt fluttering around her ankles as the early autumn breeze played with the material.

''Are you all right?'' she asked as she reached where he stood on the edge of the old family cemetery.

Although Chance and Lana had seen each other on the day he'd arrived back into town, that moment had been brief and Chance had immediately had to deal with funeral arrangements for his father.

''Sure, I'm fine.'' He willed away any lingering emotion that had momentarily gripped him. There was no way he'd show anyone the feelings that had possessed him since coming back to this ranch.

She moved closer, near enough that he caught the scent of her, a wild floral fragrance that stirred old memories. She'd worn that particular perfume years ago, when he'd first met her at the Colton ranch, where Chance had lived for a year when he'd been sixteen and Lana had been thirteen.

Someplace in the back of his mind he registered that she had grown up to be a lovely woman. Her Mexican heritage was evident in the raven-black of her hair and the darkness of her eyes. It was a quiet, understated beauty she didn't try to emphasize with an abundance of makeup.

Chance once again focused on the mound of dirt

before them. "How did you put up with him?" he asked, then looked at her again.

Her full lips curved just a bit into a half smile. "I'm a nurse, Chance. I'm accustomed to dealing with difficult patients."

"If I know my father, he was worse than difficult."

She nodded, not denying his words. "Yes, there were days he was worse than difficult, but most of the time he was too ill to be much of a bother to anyone." She placed a slender hand on his arm. "I heard about the will."

He looked at her in surprise. He'd only learned about the terms of his father's will no more than half an hour ago. It was what had driven him out of the house and here, to his father's side to curse the man who had given him life.

"Walter Bishop might be a fine lawyer, but he sometimes talks too much," she said, referring to the man who had been one of Tom Reilly's few friends and the family lawyer. "But don't worry," she hurriedly added. "As far as I know, he only talked to me. He assumed I already knew what Tom had done in the will."

"I didn't want this place anyway," Chance said, anger welling up once again as he recognized the partial lie in his own words. "Hell, it would take months of work to repair everything and get it back into good shape."

He hadn't wanted to live on the ranch ever again. Too many bad memories resided here. But he'd assumed he'd inherit the ranch, then fix it up and sell it and finally start a business of his own.

Lana dropped her hand from his arm. "But your father's will doesn't preclude you from inheriting it."

"According to the will, I have to be married in order to inherit. Here's a news flash for you, Lana— I'm not married. I never intend to be married, so it looks like this place will go to charity instead of to me."

He swept a hand through his hair and drew a deep breath. "What about you? What are you going to do now that my father is gone?"

"I need to pack up some things that are still here, then I'll go back to my apartment in town and wait for another job."

Lana had been living on the Reilly ranch for the past six months, ever since Tom suffered the first of a series of strokes. "If you need references, you know I'll be glad to write you up something," he said.

She nodded and he noticed a strand of her thick, black hair had escaped from the bun at the nape of her neck. It looked silky soft as it blew across the side of her face. "What are you going to do now?" she asked.

He shrugged. "Go back to the life I've been living." Before this moment, he thought he loved his life.

Selling farm equipment around the country, he traveled most of the time, never calling any one place home. He'd become adept at finding the best food, the nicest rooms in the small towns he traveled to, and never had a problem finding a warm, willing woman for a night's pleasure.

At the moment he felt nothing but weariness as he

thought of going back to that particular lifestyle. "How's your family?" he asked, stalling the moment he'd have to return to the house and all the memories that resided within those four walls. "It was nice of your parents to come today. Are they still working for the Coltons?"

"Yes, I can't imagine them doing anything else. Mama and Dad love the Colton family." A tiny frown appeared in the center of her forehead.

"But…?"

She shook her head as if to dismiss whatever thought had caused the wrinkle to appear. "Maya got married. She married Drake Colton."

"Really?" The news surprised Chance.

"Yes, and they have a beautiful six-month-old baby girl."

"So that makes you an aunt," he said.

"Yes, it does." She smiled, as if being an aunt pleased her immensely.

The mention of marriage once again stirred his anger. He turned toward the house. "Guess I'd better get back inside." He took several steps, but paused as she once again placed a hand on his arm.

"Wait," she said. He turned and faced her expectantly, surprised to see a faint blush of color on her cheeks. "Your father's will…it just says you have to be married to inherit. It doesn't say anything about you having to stay married, right?"

"Yeah, so all I need is a temporary wife. You know anyone who might want to apply for the job?" he asked sarcastically.

The pink of her cheeks deepened. "Me."

Surprise swept through him and he stared at her wordlessly for a long moment. "Don't be ridiculous," he finally scoffed and started to walk again.

She quickly fell in beside him, her long legs almost matching his stride. "Why is it ridiculous?" she asked. "This ranch should be yours, Chance. I'll do it, I'll be your temporary wife so you can inherit."

He stopped walking and turned to her once again, utterly bewildered by her offer. "And why would you do something like that? What do you get out of the bargain?"

Maybe she figured to marry him then when he sold the ranch she'd get half the profit, he thought. What other possible reason could she have for suggesting such a crazy scheme?

She drew a deep breath and he was suddenly aware of the press of her shapely breasts against the silk material of her white blouse. "A baby."

"A baby?" he echoed with shock. "My God, Lana, if that's what you want, fall in love and get married, have babies and live happily ever after."

She frowned. "Chance, I'm thirty-one years old. I'm not dating anyone and I have no plans to marry, but I want a child." She raised her chin as her dark gaze held his and in the depths of her dark eyes he saw her strength. The same strength he'd always found attractive in her in years past.

"Lana—"

"Think about it, Chance," she continued, her low voice ringing with a surprising boldness. "It would be perfect. We get married. You get your ranch and

I get pregnant. Once we both have what we want, we divorce. No strings attached, no messy emotions.''

Chance shook his head, trying to reconcile the woman before him with the shy, sweet young girl who'd been his confidante in one of the most difficult years of his life.

''Lana, I appreciate the offer, but I think working for my father these last few months has made you plumb loco. I can't marry you.'' He didn't intend to marry anyone. Again anger tore at him—anger at his father, who was, even from the grave, attempting to pull strings to control his life.

''It's a crazy idea and this is the end of this discussion.'' Without waiting for her reply, he stalked toward the house and the waiting guests.

She was crazy, she must be crazy to have even suggested such an idea. Lana's cheeks burned hot with humiliation as she followed Chance toward the house.

What had she been thinking? What had possibly possessed her to suggest such a thing? Chance disappeared into the front door of the house, but Lana stopped on the porch, not wanting to return to the crowd inside until she was completely composed and the warmth of her embarrassment wasn't shining on her cheeks.

She sank down into one of the two wicker rockers. She knew what she'd been thinking when she'd made the offer. She'd been thinking of the sweet baby scent of her niece, of the cuddly warmth of her in Lana's arms. Since the time of Marissa's birth, Lana had been filled with a yearning for her own baby.

Being over thirty and with no man in her life, she had heard the faint ticking of her biological clock more than once on a lonely night.

Before she'd heard about the terms of Tom Reilly's will, she'd been thinking about artificial insemination. Becoming a single parent didn't frighten her. In the best of worlds, she would have met and married a man who loved her and whom she loved, but in the real world, there was no hint of any prospective husband on the horizon.

The moment she'd heard about Chance's problem, she'd gotten the idea of a temporary marriage with him. She wanted desperately to be a mother, and who better to be the father than a man like Chance, a man who would never settle down, never demand an active role in the baby's life. Chance would be a perfect sperm donor.

She tried not to think about how many nights in her youth she had dreamed about Chance Reilly, how many hours of those youthful days she'd wasted fantasizing about the handsome brown-haired young man whose green eyes had burned with the fierce intensity of tumultuous emotions.

Silly dreams and ridiculous fantasies, she now thought. She'd long ago outgrown the crush she'd once had on Chance Reilly. Chance was every teenage girl's heartthrob but he was not the material for everlasting love.

She stood, knowing she needed to get back inside. Before she'd left the house to seek out Chance, she'd been serving as an unofficial hostess. And if she knew her mother, Inez Ramirez would be in the kitchen, washing up after everyone and replenishing the food on the dining room table.

Shoving aside her conversation with Chance, she went back inside the house. Chance stood near the dining room table, talking with several of the other ranchers in the area who had shown up to pay their respects.

There was no denying that time had only increased the man's attractiveness. His brown hair was now sun-streaked with gleaming blond strands, the variegated color only appearing to deepen the hazel green of his eyes. Time had only seemed to better define the lines of his square face, his strong nose and full lips. The shoulders that had seemed broad before now seemed impossibly so.

She consciously tore her gaze from him and headed for the kitchen. Sure enough, her mother was there, standing at the sink with her arms half-buried in soap suds.

"Mama, you don't have to do this," Lana protested.

Inez flashed her daughter a warm smile. "I don't mind. Chance has nobody else to help out."

Lana picked up a dish towel and took a plate from her mother to dry. For a moment, the two women worked in a companionable silence.

Lana fought the impulse to tell her mother what she'd just offered Chance. She knew instinctively that her mother would never understand. Lana's parents had married for love, and that love had not weakened through the years, but had rather strengthened. Inez would never understand her daughter settling for less than true love.

"And so your work here is done," Inez said as she finished the last of the dishes.

Lana nodded. "I'll pack up my things and move back to my apartment this evening." The sooner the better, she thought to herself. She wasn't particularly eager to face Chance again. Funny, but she wasn't particularly eager to move back to her silent, empty apartment, either.

Within thirty minutes her parents had left and Lana excused herself from the remaining crowd to go to the room she had called home for the past six months.

It was a small room right next door to the master bedroom. It had been Jim Hastings, one of the local doctors, who had set up the arrangement for a home nurse for Tom Reilly.

Despite the fact that a series of strokes had left him partially paralyzed, Tom refused to be hospitalized, and also refused to call his only son home to take care of him.

She lost track of time as she folded clothes and carefully placed them in her suitcase. No matter how difficult the patient, there was always an edge of sadness inside her when one finally succumbed to death.

When she had all her clothes packed, she remembered she'd left a book she'd been reading in Tom's bedroom where she'd spent long hours sitting by his bedside.

As she walked down the short hallway between the

small bedroom and the master, she realized the house had grown silent and night had fallen completely.

A small lamp burned on the table next to the bed. No ghost of Tom Reilly haunted the room. Tom had been hospitalized the day before his death. Lana had remained here, hoping he would rally and be returned to his home, but it had not been so.

She grabbed the book from the stand and stood for a moment, staring at the bed as she said a silent prayer for Tom Reilly's soul. He had not been a pleasant man and she had a feeling he could use all the prayers that were offered on his behalf.

"I'll bet he's barking orders in hell right about now."

Lana jumped in surprise and whirled toward the window, where she spied Chance sitting in the shadows of the room. "You scared me half to death," she exclaimed and clapped the paperback book over her breast to still her thudding heart.

"Sorry," he said.

"I just came in for my book," she explained. "I'm all packed, so I guess I'll just say goodbye." She turned to leave, but stopped in the doorway as he softly called her name.

"Have a cup of coffee with me." He stood and approached her, stopping just before he got close enough to invade her personal space.

In the dimness of the room, his features looked stark, taut with tension. "Everyone else has gone home and now the house seems so quiet…" His voice trailed off.

"I'd like a cup of coffee before I leave," she said

softly. Although Chance had always professed to hate his father, Lana remembered a time when all Chance had wanted was a kind touch, a word of encouragement and a simple acknowledgment of affection from the man.

There must be a small part of him that was grieving, and Lana couldn't walk away despite the fact that she still was embarrassed by her earlier outburst.

She turned and left the room, conscious of him just behind her as they walked down the hall toward the living room and kitchen.

When she'd first moved in here, she'd been struck by how plain, how austere the place was. Each room held the utilitarian furniture necessary, but little else. There were no floral arrangements, no little knick-knacks, no pictures or personal items to make the house feel like a home.

In the kitchen, she sat at the table and watched as Chance made coffee. At some point during the evening, he'd taken off his suit jacket and rolled up the sleeves of his white shirt, exposing tanned, muscled forearms.

She searched for something to say to break the silence, but her usual shyness rose up to hinder any efforts she might make toward conversation.

He didn't speak until he placed a cup of coffee before her. "Cream or sugar?" he asked.

She shook her head. "No, this is fine."

He poured himself a cup, then joined her at the table. "I haven't had a chance to thank you for all you did for Sarge," he said.

She shrugged. "I was just doing my job." She

cleared her throat, desperately wanting to fill the silence that once again fell between them. "I understand you travel a lot with your job."

He nodded, the overhead kitchen light gleaming on the sun-kissed strands of his hair. "I'm usually on the road six days of the week."

He leaned back in his chair, for the first time since arriving home he looked relaxed. "I love it. No ties, no binds, new places and new faces all the time. I spent the first twenty years of my life trying to please Sarge, now I please nobody but myself."

Although he appeared to be relaxed, Lana felt the tension that rolled from him, saw the sparks of anger that still torched the depths of his eyes.

"Then I guess you don't care that this place will all go to charity," she said.

He sat back up, his gaze burning into hers. "Yes, I care." He pushed away from the table and stood, then drew a deep breath and raked a hand through his collar-length hair as if to steady himself.

"Even though the last thing I ever want to do is ranch, and despite the fact that this place holds only terrible memories, I wanted it." His voice was low, deep with barely suppressed emotion. "I wanted to sell this place and take the money and start my own business. He owed me this, Lana. Damn him, he owed me this."

She heard the pain beneath the anger, and her heart ached for him. "Then take it," she said with the bravado that was uncharacteristic. "Marry me and claim the ranch. Fix it up and sell it. Give me a baby, then ride off into the sunset with everyone happy."

He sat down once again and eyed her incredulously. "You're serious about this."

"I've never been more serious in my life," she said truthfully. From the instant she'd heard about Chance's dilemma with his father's will, she'd felt as if a bargain between them was predestined.

"But you understand if you want a baby, that means we'd have to—we would be…" He allowed his voice to trail off.

"Chance, I know how babies are made," she said as a surge of heat suffused her cheeks.

"And that doesn't bother you—the idea of, uh, sleeping with me?"

"Of course not," she replied briskly, not quite meeting his gaze.

"Lana, I respect your parents. It wouldn't be right to them."

She offered him a small smile. "I'm not asking you to sleep with them." Her smile fell away, and she eyed him levelly. "My parents will respect my choice, my decision."

He sighed and frowned thoughtfully. "I could pay you. If we decide to do this, I could give you some of the money from the sale of this place."

She shook her head. "I don't want your money." She forced herself to look at him once again. "That wouldn't feel right. Besides, I don't need your money. All I want is a child. You give me a baby and I'll consider us even."

His forehead wrinkled with thought. "It would take a lot of work to get this place ready to put on the market." His frown deepened. "I'd want to fix it up to get top market value. According to Walt Bishop, I've got five days to fulfill the terms of the will. That means we'd have to get married within the next five days.''

A shiver of apprehension swept through Lana as she realized he was actually considering her proposal. "All we need is a license and a justice of the peace," she replied.

"Okay," he said. "You need a baby and I need a temporary wife. How about we tie the knot in two days?''

Again a tinge of anxiety whispered through her. Was this what she wanted? She thought of baby Marissa cooing to her, tiny fingers grasping around hers, and her heart constricted with deep yearning.

If she waited for nature to take its course, waited for love to find her and a traditional wedding to occur, she might wait forever.

"Two days sound fine," she said, shoving any lingering doubts to the farthest reaches of her mind.

They agreed to meet for the marriage license first thing in the morning, and moments later Lana was on her way back to her apartment.

As she drove through the September night from the Reilly ranch to her place, her head spun with what she'd just agreed to do. In two days' time she was going to become Mrs. Chance Reilly.

"And that doesn't bother you—the idea of sleeping with me?''

Chance's words played again in her head. She tightened her hands on the steering wheel.

Bother her? Yes, it bothered her. The idea of sleeping with Chance quickened her heartbeat, weakened her knees and filled her with a fiery heat. How many women got the opportunity, as adults, to fulfill what had been a forbidden adolescent fantasy?

But it wasn't quite her fantasy, she thought. In her youthful fantasy she and Chance had been desperately in love. They had tied the knot of love that would make them a forever kind of couple. That had been her fantasy at one time in her life. But what they had just discussed had nothing to do with fantasy. What they had just agreed to had absolutely nothing to do with forever.

Two

Her wedding day.

Lana stood next to Chance and tightly clasped the small bouquet Chance had surprised her with when he'd arrived at her apartment. She felt both hot and cold at the same time, and knew it was nerves that made her feel vaguely ill.

Was she doing the right thing? She was agreeing to a loveless marriage for the sake of making a baby. Yet, as she thought of her baby niece and imagined a baby of her own, she shoved all doubts from her mind.

She swallowed hard as the justice of the peace cleared his throat and began the ceremony that would make Chance and Lana man and wife.

No traditional wedding gown and tux for this couple. Lana wore a pale pink dress and Chance wore a brown suit that emphasized the golden streaks in his hair and the deep green of his eyes.

They had invited no family members to see their exchange of vows. Both of them understood their wedding was not a cause for celebration, but rather a bargain made between two consenting adults. A business deal of sorts.

"Are you sure about this?" Chance asked beneath his breath as the justice of the peace spoke of commitment and the bonds of matrimony. She hesitated only a moment, then nodded.

One corner of Chance's mouth turned up and for just a moment his eyes sparkled with amusement. "And you promise me your daddy is not going to come after me with a shotgun when this is all over?"

Grateful for his smile, she quickly returned it and felt an easing of the tension between them. "I promise," she replied.

She had spent the most difficult hour of her life the day before with her mother and father, telling them she was marrying Chance in order to help him gain his inheritance. She didn't tell them what she intended to get out of the arrangement. She felt a little guilty in that she suspected her parents assumed this would be a marriage in name only for the sole purpose of helping Chance.

Even knowing this marriage was hardly a marriage at all, Lana couldn't help the way her heart thundered as the justice of the peace spoke the words that bound her, at least temporarily, to Chance.

Practically in the blink of an eye, the brief ceremony was over and Chance was instructed to kiss his bride. Again Lana's heart bumped against her ribs as it beat too fast, too hard.

He bent his head and she closed her eyes. His lips barely brushed against hers, a brief dance of warmth there only a second, then gone.

"Let's get out of here," he murmured.

Lana chided herself for her momentary disappointment. What had she expected? That he'd wrap his arms around her, gaze deeply into her eyes, then kiss her with a passion that would steal her breath away? Not in this lifetime, she chided herself, and certainly not in this marriage.

"We need to get over to Walter Bishop's office and give him a copy of the marriage certificate," Chance said the moment they left.

They got into Chance's sports car and headed for the lawyer's office. Lana tried to think of something, anything, to say, but Chance's silence and his stony expression deterred her.

She hadn't asked him about girlfriends. Was it possible he had a special somebody back in Wichita? He'd said he never intended to get married, but that didn't mean he didn't have a significant other.

She frowned. If he did have somebody special in his life, why wasn't she sitting in this car with him now? She suddenly realized she knew little about the man she had just married.

She'd known him as an angry, troubled sixteen-year-old who had been sent to the Coltons for a year of foster care in an effort to cool down the heat between him and his father. But Lana didn't really know what kind of man Chance had become in the intervening years.

"This will just take a minute," Chance said as he pulled up to the curb before Bishop's law office. "You want to come in or wait here?"

"I'll wait here," she said, then hurriedly added, "unless you'd like me to come in."

He frowned. "I'll be right back." He got out of the car and disappeared into the building without a backward glance.

Lana stared down at the bouquet in her lap and tried to still the nerves that still jangled inside her. She'd performed her end of the bargain and she assumed that later tonight Chance would do his part to fulfill his end of their pact.

Tonight she was going to make love with Chance. Tonight she was going to make love for the very first time in her life. Again a cold wave swept through her at the same time a flush of heat rose inside. She had never been so nervous in her entire life.

Think about the end result, she told herself. Don't be nervous, just concentrate on the fact that nine months from tonight you might be holding a beautiful baby of your own. Her heart swelled at the thought.

Lana had always wanted children, but since her niece's birth her want had grown into something much bigger. She was a nurturer at heart, and longed to nurture her own child.

She jumped as Chance opened his car door and slid back behind the wheel. "Everything all right?" she asked.

"Fine. Walter says it will take several weeks for

everything to be signed, sealed and delivered. In the meantime, I've got a lot of work ahead of me at the ranch.''

It was just after two in the afternoon when they pulled into the Reilly ranch. Immediately Chance disappeared down the hall and into the bedroom, and Lana stood uncertainly in the kitchen, wondering what would happen next.

Would he want to make love right away? With the midday sun shining through the windows? Her cheeks burned at the very thought. She'd certainly prefer the darkness of night for her first foray into the act of lovemaking.

She whirled around as he came back into the kitchen, surprised to see that he had changed out of his suit and into a pair of worn jeans and a black T-shirt.

''I'm going to do a little work out in the barn,'' he said, his gaze not quite meeting hers. ''I'll be back in later.'' Before the words had completely left his mouth he was gone, disappearing out the back door.

Lana remained standing in the center of the kitchen for a long moment. She knew it was ridiculous to feel neglected, to feel cast aside and unloved.

She was unloved, at least as far as Chance Reilly was concerned. She was a necessity in his life at the moment and it was stupid to get her feelings hurt just because he'd hightailed it out of the house to work in the barn on their wedding day.

She went into the bedroom—the master bedroom where she would be spending the night with Chance. She'd spent the day before bringing more of her things over from her apartment, and Chance had spent part of the day transforming the room from Sarge's to his own.

A new multicolored bedspread covered crisp new sheets. The spread was a splash of color in an otherwise colorless room, but she knew it was Chance's need to brand the room with something of his own.

The top of the dresser held an array of items— several bottles of cologne, small change and a pack of matches from a café in Topeka, Kansas, with a phone number written in pencil across the front.

Lana was certain it was a woman's number. Chance probably had a woman waiting for him in every city when he traveled. And why wouldn't he? He was handsome and incredibly sexy and had just enough bad-boy aura about him to make him wonderfully intriguing. Women would be drawn to him like bees to honey.

She took off her dress and exchanged it for a pair of jeans and a long-sleeved, rose-colored blouse at the same time wondering how long Chance would remain outside. Would he work all afternoon, or come back inside in an hour or two?

Carrying her wedding bouquet back into the kitchen, she contemplated how to spend the afternoon. She was now a wife, and the least she could do was make a nice meal for her husband.

She was eager for any activity that would take her mind away from the night to come, a night that could be beautiful beyond her wildest dreams…or confirm to her that she'd made the biggest mistake in her life.

*   *   *

Chance banged another nail into the barn door, using more force than was necessary to drive it into the slightly rotten wood.

He didn't know what to do with his anger. It had been a living, breathing force inside him since he'd arrived back here and found his father had passed away. It had built to mammoth proportions when he'd heard about the terms of the will, threatening to consume him entirely.

He paused in his task and sat on a nearby bale of musty-smelling hay. The barn was a wreck, filled with cast-off machinery and rotting hay and feed. The corral outside was falling down. Fences needed mending, boards needed replacing. The entire place showed more than one year of neglect.

"And now it's mine," he said aloud and felt a momentary surge of triumph. He'd beaten Sarge. Despite his father's efforts, he'd succeeded in inheriting the place that he'd always told himself he hated.

And now what he felt more than anything was guilt as he thought of the woman who had agreed to be his "bride." The passing years had been good to Lana. She had only grown more lovely than he remembered. She deserved more than a temporary husband and single parenthood.

He plucked a piece of hay from the bale and worried it between his fingers, his mind racing back in time, remembering the thirteen-year-old Lana who had befriended the troubled, raging sixteen-year-old he had been.

Even then, at that young age, Lana had emitted a quiet strength, a sweet nature and a sympathetic ear that had drawn him to her despite their three-year age difference. For the year of their friendship, Chance had found a soothing of his anger, a calming of his pain.

In the years since, he'd always entertained a fond gratitude for the young girl who had been his confidante and support for that year of his life.

And how had he repaid her? By agreeing to her crazy idea. She'd fulfilled her end of the bargain and tonight he must fulfill his.

For the first time in his life, something he enjoyed doing, something he'd been told he was quite good at, suddenly seemed daunting. Tonight he had to make love to Lana.

He tossed the broken piece of hay aside and stood once again. Grabbing another handful of nails, he began hammering, at the same time his mind whirled with thoughts of the night to come.

No safe sex tonight. Pregnancy was the desired aftermath. In all his adult life, in all his physical relationships, he'd always been extremely careful to make sure there was not a baby as a result of a night of passion.

Chance had absolutely no desire to be a father. The very idea filled him with anxiety. What he'd learned from his own father's parenting he never wanted to pass on to anyone else.

But Lana didn't want a father for her baby, he reminded himself. All she wanted was a sperm donor. He was surprised to realize the whole idea of sleeping with Lana made him nervous.

What if he couldn't fulfill his end of their bargain?

What if he couldn't perform? He shoved this thought away, knowing if he dwelled on it, he would certainly have a problem when the time came.

Dusk was falling when he made his way back to the house. As he walked into the back door, the mouth-watering scent of roast beef greeted him.

Lana was not in the kitchen, but the table was set for two. He grunted in surprise as he saw that someplace she had dug up a bright yellow tablecloth, and in the center of the table her simple wedding bouquet had been transformed into a sweet-smelling table centerpiece.

A woman's touch.

A sudden memory flitted through his mind, a distant memory of a blond-haired woman arranging flowers in the center of the table, of her laughter that was bright as sunshine as the scent of rich chocolate chip cookies wafted from the oven.

The memory of his mother stabbed through him. When she'd died, she'd taken all the softness, all the nurturing, all the woman's touches from this house and from his life.

Lana's efforts found the hidden place of neglect in his soul and stirred something warm. He turned as she came into the kitchen.

"Oh, you're back," she said.

He nodded, suddenly feeling guilty for running out on her, escaping to do work the moment they'd returned home. He gestured toward the table. "Looks like you've been busy."

Her forehead wrinkled worriedly. "I hope you

don't mind. I found the tablecloth in a drawer and thought it would be nice.''

''It is nice,'' he assured her and was rewarded by a slight blush of pleasure coloring her cheeks.

''I made supper. It's ready whenever you are.'' He could tell she was nervous by the way her gaze refused to meet his and the slight catch in her breath as she spoke.

''I need to shower, then I'll be ready to eat.'' He smiled at her in an attempt to diffuse some of the tension. ''I'll be out in about fifteen minutes or so.''

He left her standing in the kitchen. A moment later he stood beneath the hot spray of water in the shower, trying not to think of the nighttime to come.

Instead he focused on all the work that would have to be done on the ranch in order to get it ready for sale. It was an awesome task, but the reward would be awesome as well. His father had owed no mortgage, so the land and the house were free and clear of debt.

He could afford to hire several men to help him get the place in shape. He'd go into town tomorrow and see about hiring help. With several ranch hands, the work would go quickly and he could have the place on the market in no time.

Finishing his shower, he then towel dried and dressed in a clean pair of jeans and a button-down sports shirt. When he entered the kitchen the homey scene before him again struck him.

Lana, apparently unaware of him standing in the doorway, was at the oven. For a moment he stood silent, merely admiring her backside. She'd been slender as a young girl, and she had retained that long-legged, coltish slenderness.

Despite her slenderness, there was no mistaking the gentle curve of her hips, the shapeliness of her buttocks in the tight jeans.

Her dark hair was as he'd always seen it, tucked into a neat bun at the nape of her neck, a single errant strand loose and without restraint. He wondered what it would look like completely freed and flowing down her back. He wondered what it would feel like cascading against his fingertips.

She turned at that moment, a bowl of steaming mashed potatoes in her hands. She jumped in surprise and juggled the bowl precariously before finally settling it on the edge of the table. "You scared me," she exclaimed.

"Sorry," he replied. "Is there anything I can do to help?" Domesticity wasn't exactly his style, but he felt a sudden desire to do something with her, some tiny act that might break the thickness of the air between them.

"There's a salad in the fridge. If you want to get that on the table, I'll get the roast and gravy," she said.

Within minutes they were seated across from each other, eating the best meal Chance could ever remember enjoying. Still, the air was thick, the tension palpable as the shadows outside the kitchen window deepened, portending the coming of night.

He should have taken her right to the bedroom the moment the ceremony was over earlier in the day. Then, the act would be over, the ice would be broken and they wouldn't be suffering the taut tension that was like a third guest at the table.

Dinner consisted of strained small talk, and Chance was almost grateful when the meal was over and the dishes had been washed and put away.

Chance went outside to make sure everything was locked up and secure for the night, then returned to the house, where Lana sat on the edge of the sofa looking as if she wanted nothing more than to bolt.

Enough was enough, he thought. "I'm going to bed," he said, and watched as her dark eyes flared slightly. "You can join me whenever you're ready." He hesitated a moment, then added, "Unless you want to call this whole thing off."

Her eyes snapped brightly and she jumped to her feet. "Not on your life, Chance Reilly," she said with a burst of unexpected spirit. "I did my part. I'm not about to run before you do yours." With these words, she stalked past him and disappeared into the bathroom.

Chance stared after her. For a moment, just a brief moment, he thought he saw not dread or anxiety in her eyes, but rather excitement and anticipation.

A stir of excitement sang through him in response, the excitement of taking a new lover, the anticipatory thrill of discovery.

He turned out all the lights in the living room and went into the bedroom where the faint bedside lamp spilled a whisper of golden light through the room. Undressing, he tried not to think about the young, sweet girl Lana had been and instead focused on the fact that she was an attractive thirty-one-year-old woman.

Naked, he slid in beneath the crisp cotton sheets and waited. Staring up at the ceiling, he concentrated on what he would do with the money from the sale of the ranch. First and foremost, he wanted to start his own business. He wasn't sure exactly what kind of business it would be, but the important thing would be he'd enjoy being his own boss.

He'd get a condo, something low-maintenance but nice. And then there was a Harley he'd been contemplating. It was a sleek, chrome machine he could easily imagine riding on his days off.

A noise at the doorway diverted his attention from the ceiling, and when he saw Lana standing there, all thoughts of condos and motorcycles fled his mind.

Clad in a white nightgown that clung to her breasts, then fell in a soft cascade to her bare feet, she looked like a vision from a dream. A very good dream.

Her glorious hair was loose and fell below her shoulders like a cloak of black silk, and Chance's fingers itched with the need to tangle themselves in it.

She said nothing as she moved to the side of the bed and slid in beneath the covers. She lay flat on her back, barely taking up any space on the large mattress.

Chance raised himself up on one elbow and smiled. "This is very awkward, isn't it?"

His words seemed to chisel away some of the tension. She smiled. "Horribly awkward," she agreed.

"We can take this very slow," he said. He reached

out and lightly touched her cheek. Her skin was softer than he'd imagined and a spark of desire began to glow deep inside him.

"Slow. I'd like that." Her voice was a bare whisper as his fingers moved from her cheek and instead trailed down the curve of her jaw.

He'd worried that he wouldn't feel the necessary desire to fulfill his end of the bargain, but as his fingers touched the silk of her hair, and her breathing quickened slightly, he knew there would be no problem where desire was concerned.

He bent and touched his lips to hers and her instantaneous response delighted him. He'd been afraid that Lana would be overly shy and self-conscious as a lover, but her kiss was filled with sweet heat that further fed the spark inside him.

He deepened the kiss with his tongue and she responded, opening her mouth to him as her arms reached up to clasp him around the neck.

Moving his body closer to hers, he was enveloped by the evocative scent of her perfume and could feel her body heat radiating outward as if to warm him.

His mouth left hers and traveled the path his fingers had trailed earlier...down her jawline, then lingering in the vulnerable flesh just beneath her ear where a pulse beat rapidly. Her arms tightened in response to his nipping, teasing kisses.

His fingers toyed with the ribbon between her breasts, but he carefully kept away from a more intimate touch, knowing it was too soon. Instead he claimed her mouth once again, enjoying the way she tasted and the way her tongue thrust and parried with his own.

All too quickly, mere kissing wasn't enough. Chance wanted, needed to touch her, feel her warm skin against his, cup her bare breasts in his hands.

He stroked his hands down the length of her sides. He could tell she was ready for him to take them into the next dimension. Her breathing had grown more rapid and occasionally a tiny moan issued from her lips.

"Lana," he whispered softly. "I want to take your gown off."

In the pale illumination of the room, she gazed at him, and he saw her desire in the dark depths of her eyes. "Shut off the light," she replied breathlessly.

He hesitated. He didn't want the light off. He wanted to see the beautiful skin he was eager to caress. He wanted to see her breasts, the flat of her stomach, the curve of her hips and the length of her legs.

"Please, Chance," she said as if recognizing his hesitation. "We can keep the light on next time."

He acquiesced to her wishes with the promise of another time ringing in his ears. Turning out the light, he heard the whisper of silk leaving flesh and when he reached for her again, she was warm and naked in his arms.

Any further conscious thought was impossible as his hands stroked her heated flesh and she returned his touch, caress for caress. Their mouths found each other's as they explored one another's bodies, finding the magical, secret places that evoked sighs or sweet shudders of pleasure.

All too quickly, Chance was ready to possess her completely. She arched beneath him and a deep, throaty moan escaped her as he moved between her thighs.

He moved partially into her and encountered resistance. He pressed deeper, harder, and instantly her fingernails bit into the flesh of his back. He froze, recognizing suddenly what the resistance had been.

"Lana." Her name was both a protest and a plea. He started to pull away, shock riveting through him as he realized what he'd done, realized she'd been a virgin.

"No, Chance. It's all right. Don't stop now. Please don't stop." The fingers that had bitten into him now pulled him closer.

Heaven help him, he didn't want to stop. She surrounded him, warm and tight and achingly pleasurable. Still, he remained inert, afraid of hurting her any more than he just had.

"Please don't stop," she repeated, the words a warm breath in his neck and followed by the press of her lips against his skin.

He moved tentatively, gently against her, awed by the gift she'd just given him and at the same time angry that she hadn't told him beforehand.

Had he known she'd never been with a man before, he would have never agreed to this whole scheme. Now it was too late. In a single moment he'd transformed her, changed her forever, and she would never again be the same woman she'd been before climbing into his bed.

Had he known she had never made love before, he would have taken more time, enjoyed introducing her to sensations that would be new and exciting.

But it was too late now. Buried deep within her, he couldn't staunch the storm of passion that coursed through him. Like a tidal wave, he was helpless in the wake of it as he felt himself building to a summit. Then he was over the summit and crashing down as he hoarsely cried out her name.

Moments later, he lay on his back, trying to catch his breath and wondering how on earth a woman who had never made love before had managed to get him to such a fever pitch.

He heard the slide of silk fabric and realized she had grabbed her nightgown and was once again pulling it on. "Lana, why didn't you tell me?" he asked with a touch of censure in his voice. "I would have never agreed to any of this had I known."

"That's why I didn't tell you. I'm tired, Chance. We'll talk about it tomorrow." The mattress shook with her movements and he sensed she'd turned her back to him.

A momentary urge to reach out and touch her, to pull her into his arms and hold her swept through him. It surprised him, the need to gather her against him and feel her heartbeat against his own.

But he dismissed the impulse. It was obvious she wasn't interested in sharing any afterglow with him. She was finished with him now that the deed had been done.

As he stared up at the dark ceiling, he reminded himself that she was nothing to him but a means to an end. And it was apparent that he was the same to her. That was just fine with him. The last thing he wanted was any sort of emotional tie to this woman or this place.

In three to five months time, he'd be out of here and this time when he left Prosperino, he didn't intend to ever look back.

A dream awakened Emily Blair Colton. She sat straight up in bed, heart pounding with the residual terror of the dream. No, not a dream, a nightmare.

She stared around the room, looking for something familiar, safe. Bright moonlight streamed into the bedroom window, painting the room in silvery shades.

A deep, abiding sadness stole away the terror as reality sank in. She wasn't home. She wasn't safe and sound at the ranch in Prosperino, California, with her loving adoptive parents, Meredith and Joe Colton.

She was in the small town of Red River, Montana, hiding out because somebody was trying to kill her. Chilled, and with the memory of the dream further haunting her, she got out of bed, grabbed her robe and left the bedroom.

She turned on the table lamp, pulled her robe on, then sank down on the sofa, her mind in a jumble of thoughts just as it had been for the last year, since leaving home and running for her life.

Raking a trembling hand through her hair, she

thought of the dream she'd just had. It was a familiar vision that haunted her more and more frequently.

It always began the same. She and her mother, Meredith, were in the car. In the dream, Emily was no longer twenty, but rather eleven years old and filled with the joy and security of Meredith's love, love that in a screech of twisting metal and the tinkling of shattered glass had evaporated.

It was never the car accident in the dream that frightened Emily, rather it was always what happened after the wreck that ripped terror through her soul.

Dazed by a head wound, bleeding and frightened, Emily had opened her eyes to see two identical mommies. They had the exact same hair, the exact same features, but one was Emily's loving, beautiful mother and the other was a mother with hard, gleaming eyes and a wicked, hateful smile. And in the blink of an eye, the good mommy was gone, replaced by the bad mommy.

It had only been in the past year that Emily had begun to realize that the visions that tormented her in her dreams were not really dreams, but rather memories of the events that had occurred on that fateful day of the accident.

And now, almost ten years after the day of that accident, Emily knew the truth. Meredith's wicked, evil twin sister, Patsy, had usurped not only Meredith's identity, but her home and her family as well.

Grief ripped through Emily as she thought of the years lost, of the family that had disintegrated beneath the dramatic changes in "Meredith."

But now Emily knew the truth, the whole truth. The

Meredith she'd lost on the day of the accident was in Jackson, Mississippi, trying desperately to regain the memory she'd lost that day.

Once Dr. Wilkes helped the real Meredith cope with the trauma she'd suffered, she would return home and reclaim her life.

Emily left the sofa and went to the window. Staring out into the darkness of the night, she'd never felt quite so alone.

Patsy knew Emily knew the truth and someplace out there was a hired killer whom Patsy had paid to get rid of Emily. He'd nearly succeeded twice before, but Emily had managed to escape.

She shivered, realizing the darkness outside could hide many things, including a killer with a limp and a Fu Manchu mustache and goatee. He could be out there right now, watching, waiting, eagerly plotting the perfect time to make his move on her.

She turned away from the window and shut out the light, then curled up on the sofa, her mind whirling in chaos. She had to do something about Toby. A vision of the handsome young deputy filled her head. When she'd been hiding out in Keyhole, Wyoming, Toby had not only befriended her, he'd fallen in love with her. And how she wished she loved him back... but she didn't.

The phone call she'd received several nights before replayed in her mind. Wyatt and Annie, friends she'd made while in Keyhole had called to see that she was all right, and it had been Wyatt who had told her that Toby was distraught, upset that she was gone and worried about her well-being. Wyatt had told her that

Toby had begged Wyatt to tell him where she was, but Wyatt had respected her wishes and hadn't told.

She'd disappeared from Keyhole without saying goodbye to the deputy who had cared about her, leaving him with questions and an aching heart. But, what could she do about it now? What should she do about it now?

Closing her eyes, she sent a prayer heavenward. She prayed that Meredith would regain her memory and reclaim her life and that Patsy would be arrested and put behind bars before her hired killer found this place…before he found Emily.

Three

Lana knew she was in bed alone before she opened her eyes. She felt Chance's absence. It was as if when he'd left the room, he'd taken part of the energy with him.

She opened an eye and reached out to touch the pillow that still held the depression from his head, the heat of his body.

Chance.

She closed her eyes again and thought back over what they had shared the night before.

For just a moment, as Chance had kissed her, as his hands had caressed her and made her body sing, she'd fancied herself just a tiny bit in love with him.

It had been a harmless fantasy, just a game she'd played in her mind to justify the intimacy they'd shared. But now, with the bright early-morning light shining in her eyes, reality stole the fantasy and she knew what they'd done the night before had had nothing to do with love.

In fact, she wondered if Chance was angry with her. Was that what had driven him from bed so early? She left the bed and went into the bathroom.

A moment later as she stood beneath a hot spray of water, she steeled herself for the possibility that she would have to face his ire. She certainly knew he'd been shocked to discover her a virgin. Had he also been angry with her for not telling him ahead of time?

The pain of consummation had surprised her. Even now, she was sore but knew next time would be better. Next time…the thought made a shiver of anticipation race up her spine.

She finished up her shower and dressed for the day, then went into the kitchen where she found a fresh pot of coffee, but no sign of Chance.

Maybe he wasn't mad at her. Maybe he'd just found the entire experience distasteful. A man like Chance would be used to making love to beautiful women, women who were skilled in the art of lovemaking.

He'd probably been turned off by the fact that she hadn't known where to touch him, how to kiss him in the ways he was accustomed to being touched and kissed. She had been rather clueless to the whole process of lovemaking.

She sighed and poured herself a cup of coffee and moved to the window. Instantly she spied Chance out

by the barn. He was working on the corral fencing
and even though it was early and the air was cool, he
worked bare-chested, clad only in a pair of faded,
worn jeans.

For a moment she enjoyed the opportunity of
watching him without him knowing. She could see
even from this distance the light sheen of sweat that
coated his broad chest.

The morning sun played on the golden highlights
of his hair and he looked more like a surfer than a
farm equipment salesman. He looked utterly virile,
devastatingly sexy and overwhelmingly masculine.

When he'd first arrived at the Colton ranch, sent
there to give him and his father a cooling-off period
from each other, her mother had warned her to stay
away from him.

"That boy is trouble," Inez had told her thirteen-
year-old daughter. "You can see it in his eyes. He's
mad at the entire world and heaven help anyone who
gets in his path."

And for the first couple of days Chance had been
at the ranch, Lana had done as her mother had instructed and given Chance a wide berth.

During those first days, Chance had broken the
rules, kept himself isolated from the others and wore
a chip on his shoulder the size of Los Angeles.

Then slowly, Meredith Colton's love and Joe Colton's discipline and affection began to work on him.
Some of the rage left his eyes and he broke the rules
less and less often. And it was during the next couple
of months that he and Lana formed the bonds of
friendship.

She'd discovered that beneath the rage was a gentle, caring young man who had a wonderful sense of humor and who longed to belong somewhere.

She watched him now, admiring the breadth of his shoulders, remembering how the muscles of his back had felt beneath her fingertips the night before. The muscles had felt so strong, and yet the skin covering them had been soft and warm.

Turning away from the window, she frowned and tried to shove thoughts of last night out of her mind. Sinking down at the table, she once again thought of the boy Chance had been.

During the year he'd stayed at the Coltons, he and Lana had shared many conversations. Actually, Chance had done most of the talking, sharing with her his thoughts about life, his father and girls. And in those conversations, Lana had developed a tremendous crush for the handsome boy he had been.

But that had been a long time ago, and in the intervening years she and Chance had only seen each other occasionally when he came home for a holiday.

As a young girl she'd fancied herself madly in love with Chance Reilly. And now she was married to him, had spent the night in his arms and felt as if she had no idea what kind of man he'd become.

It didn't matter what kind of man he'd become, she told herself. After all, this was just a temporary arrangement, a bargain where both got what they wanted, then said goodbye to each other. She'd promised him no binding ties, no messy emotions.

Chance remained outside for most of the day. At noon, Lana took him out a couple of sandwiches and a tall glass of iced tea, which he accepted gratefully. He ate quickly, barely speaking, then immediately went back to work.

Lana returned to the house and spent the rest of the day cleaning the house, moving the rest of her personal items from the spare room into his bedroom and preparing the evening meal.

She liked housework and enjoyed cooking, and the afternoon passed quickly as she busied herself with various chores. By the time Chance walked into the house at six o'clock, she had a hearty beef stew awaiting him and fresh bread just out of the oven.

"Lana, all this isn't necessary," he exclaimed as he washed up at the kitchen sink. "I didn't marry you in order to gain a cook and housekeeper."

"I enjoy doing it," she protested. "I've always loved to cook, but have been out of practice. It's no fun to cook just for one." She motioned him to the table, then moved to the counter to slice the hot bread. As she worked, she was aware of his gaze on her, felt it burning into her back.

She finished slicing the bread, then joined him at the table, knowing it was time to talk about what had happened the night before. "Chance, about last night..."

His eyes, so green, darkened to the color of a storm-swept sea. "You should have told me, Lana. I deserved to know the truth. I would have never agreed to this had you told me."

"And that's exactly why I didn't tell you. Besides, what difference does it make?" She raised her chin with a touch of bravado. "If it hadn't been you, it would have been somebody else. Sooner or later, it was going to happen.'' She passed him the stew bowl.

''Why hasn't it happened before?'' He took the bowl from her and for a moment concentrated on serving himself. When he looked at her again, the storms were gone and his gaze merely radiated a curiosity. ''I mean, you're a very attractive woman. I'm sure lots of men have wanted to date you, to make love to you.''

Her cheeks warmed as she took the bowl back from him and served herself. ''I haven't really dated much. I realized early on that if I wanted to go to college, the only way I'd get there was to get good enough grades to be offered a scholarship. Mom and Dad didn't have the money to send me to nursing school.''

A small smile curved the corner of Chance's mouth. ''So, you became an egghead.''

She loved that sexy half smile of his. It lit up all his features and sent a warmth into his eyes. ''Yes, I guess I became an egghead. I worked hard and studied to get A's. Then came college and nursing school and there just wasn't time for dating.''

''But you've been out of college for a long time,'' he observed.

She shrugged. ''I went right to work and there just has never seemed to be enough time to commit to any relationships.''

She couldn't tell him that part of her problem had been an innate shyness, a shyness that had made dating torturous. She wasn't good at small talk and wouldn't know how to flirt if her life depended on it. It had been easier to concentrate on her work, which had filled her life completely—at least she had believed her life fulfilled—until she'd held little Marissa in her arms.

"Anyway," she continued, "what's done is done. We're here now and I have no regrets about the bargain we made."

For a few moments they ate in silence, then he gazed at her once again. "You know, single parenthood isn't exactly a piece of cake. Just ask me. My old man certainly didn't do a bang-up job."

"I'll handle it just fine, and in any case your father probably wouldn't have been a good parent even if your mother had lived," she said softly.

He hesitated a moment, then nodded his agreement. "I used to think about that a lot," he said. "I thought if my mother had been around, she wouldn't have let him beat me or talk to me like I was a piece of dirt. Then I'd get mad at her for leaving us, even though I knew she'd had no control over her own death."

"It was easier for you to direct your anger at your mother rather than at your father. You had to deal with your father on a regular basis. Your mother was a safe object for your anger."

That half grin curved his mouth again. "Hmm, a wife, a good cook and a pop psychologist all rolled into one."

Lana blushed, wondering if he was censuring her. "I'm sorry. It's really none of my business."

He rewarded her with a full smile. "You listened to me cuss enough about it when we were younger. It should be your business."

She relaxed. "I didn't mind listening to you. You needed somebody to talk to."

"And you were so easy to talk to," he replied.

She said nothing, but she knew the truth. She'd believed herself so crazy in love with him, she'd hung on his every word, delighted in each tiny confession he'd shared with her. It had been easy to be a good listener if it meant spending time with him.

She'd known even then that part of what had made her so easy for him to talk to was that he didn't consider her a peer. She was nothing more than a sweet kid to him. She was safe, and he could say anything to her, confess anything and not lose face.

He grinned at her again. "Yeah, you were always easy to talk to, and for the most part I always trusted your advice. Until Susan Cahill."

Lana clapped a hand over her mouth to stifle a sudden giggle.

Susan Cahill. She'd been a foster child with the Coltons for a brief couple of weeks. Almost eighteen years old and stunningly beautiful, Susan had instantly been pegged by Lana as conceited and vain and utterly silly. But Chance had developed an instant case of lust for the blond-haired, blue-eyed "older" woman.

"I gave you good advice," she protested as she lowered her hand from her mouth. "How was I to know the girl had a germ fetish?" But she had known. In the single conversation Lana had shared with the girl, Lana had told her of her desire to become a nurse, and Susan had proclaimed that particular career "gross" because nurses were exposed to germs.

"There I was, feeling all sad because Susan barely looked at me, so what do I do?" He raised an eyebrow and eyed her wryly. "I went to the girl I trusted to get advice about women."

Laughter once again bubbled to Lana's lips. "And I gave you what advice I had. I figured if you sidled up next to her and told her you didn't feel so well, she would lay her hand on your forehead, offer to help you feel better."

"Yeah, and when I told her I didn't feel so well, she shoved me halfway across the pasture and told me to get the hell away from her." His laughter joined hers. "I should have known then that you were going to be a nurse. At that tender age you were already thinking of patient care."

She sobered slightly. "Susan wasn't right for you anyway."

The laughter that had rang from him stopped, and his eyes grew stormy once again. "There isn't a woman in this world right for me," he said, his voice low and edgy. "I wouldn't be in the marriage now if it wasn't a way to beat my father. I don't want to be married. I like the life I have just fine. I can't wait to sell this place and get back to it."

As he focused once again on his food, Lana wondered what had stirred his passionate outburst. Had she threatened him in some way? Did he not trust her to abide by their agreement?

It was as if he was warning her, telling her that she

shouldn't make the mistake of taking their marriage seriously.

He needn't worry. Although her heart would always maintain a little glow for the boy he had been, she had no illusions where the man and this marriage were concerned.

"Chance, when the time comes for you to walk away, nobody will hold you here."

He met her gaze once again, then nodded and returned to eating the meal. Any moment of shared laughter and warmth was gone, not even an echo lingering in the tense silence that returned.

Chance threw his sports car into fourth gear and raced down the road that eventually would take him into the town of Prosperino.

There was nothing he hated more than feeling guilty, and at the moment he was feeling damned guilty. Since the moment he and Lana had said "I do" he'd been behaving badly.

When he'd walked into the kitchen that evening, he'd been engulfed by the scents of home cooking, overwhelmed by the tiny little touches Lana had added to make the place seem more homey.

There was a part of him, a part of him that he had never before realized, that was hungry for a real home. A leftover piece from his dysfunctional childhood, he told himself.

When he'd agreed to this insane plot with Lana, he hadn't really thought it through. He'd been so angry with his father, and so eager to win, he hadn't considered how difficult it might be to live with a woman, especially this particular woman.

Lana, with her lovely dark eyes and that cascade of black hair. Lana, with her sweet smiles and an easy acceptance of each low and high point offered by life.

As a young girl, she'd been a balm to his spirit, a sympathetic ear that had offered no judgment, no censure no matter what he said.

She'd been pretty then, a shy, slender girl with big black eyes and a mane of hair. Each time he'd returned to Prosperino and had run into her, he'd been struck by how her beauty had only intensified with time.

He'd been pleasantly surprised last night by how passionately, how eagerly she had met his caresses, his kisses. He'd assumed she had experience. He frowned and tightened his fingers around the steering wheel. It had been a shock to realize she'd been a virgin.

He would not make love to her tonight. Even though she'd said nothing, he knew today she must be feeling some residual pain. He hadn't been particularly gentle until too late. He frowned irritably. What he meant was he would not have sex with her tonight. That was all it was—sex with a purpose.

What worried him most of all was that she seemed to be nesting, creating a home where none had existed in preparation for a baby, a baby he wanted no part of.

He didn't ever want to be a father. He, more than anyone, knew the needs that little kids had, needs he would never be able to meet because they'd never been met in him.

He shoved away thoughts of Lana and fatherhood as he pulled into a parking space in front of the Prosperino Café. He'd learned a long time ago on one of his few trips home that if he wanted to catch up on the gossip in the area, needed to buy or sell any kind of equipment, or simply wanted a great cup of coffee, the café was the place to come. The café had always been a favorite haunt in his childhood, a place where he had often run to escape from his father.

It was obvious he'd come in the lull between the supper rush and the late evening bunch. There were only three other patrons inside, all sitting in the same booth.

Chance slid onto one of the stools at the counter and eyed the pretty waitress he didn't know. At another time, in another place, he might have flirted with her. At this moment, in this time, the idea held little appeal.

"What can I get for you?" she asked as she drew a pad from the pocket of her apron.

"Just a cup of coffee. Is Angie still around?"

"Sure, she's in the back."

"Would you tell her Chance is here to see her?"

"No problem. I'll be right back." She whirled around and disappeared into a doorway that led to the kitchen.

A moment later a robust woman with a headful of gray hair came sweeping out, her face wreathed in a wide grin. "Chance Reilly, you devil." She faced him across the counter and grabbed his hands in hers. "Let me take a good look at you."

Chance grinned. "It's good to see you, Angie."

"And aren't you still the most handsome devil I've ever seen."

"Don't you let Harmon hear you say that, he'll take a bullwhip to me just for looking at you," Chance teased.

She laughed. "Harmon is getting so old, all he'd manage to do would be to get himself hopelessly tangled in a whip." Her smile faded and she eyed him soberly. "You doing okay? I was real sorry to hear about your daddy."

"Then you're probably the only person in town sorry to hear about him," he replied.

Angie and her husband, Harmon had worked in the café for as long as Chance could remember, and over the years the two of them had often consoled Chance when his father had driven him from the ranch.

"And what's this I hear about you tying the knot with Lana Ramirez?" Angie continued. "That had to have been the fastest courtship in the history of mankind."

"You know me, Angie. I've always been a fast worker." He and Lana had agreed that they would tell nobody the real terms of their marriage. There was only a handful of people who were privy to the terms of the will and who probably suspected an arranged marriage, but nobody would hear it from Lana or Chance. "Besides, Lana just swept me off my feet."

Angie released his hands and straightened. "I'm

glad you've finally settled down, and with a good woman, too. Don't you go breaking her heart, Chance Reilly. I'm sure you've already broken more than your share.''

Chance shifted positions on the stool, uncomfortable with the topic of conversation. ''Angie, have you heard of any good ranch hands looking for work?''

She moved aside as the waitress poured him a cup of coffee and slid it in front of him. Angie frowned thoughtfully. ''Hmm, Kirk Brighton was in here the other day looking for work. You going to take over the place and get it back into shape?''

''That's the plan,'' Chance said.

Angie nodded with a satisfied smile. ''That's good. It's a beautiful spread, but your dad's heart was never really in it, then he got so sick in the last year, he just let it all go. Besides, you belong on that ranch.''

Chance didn't tell her that he intended to sell it as soon as possible. As the talk turned to the men in the area, he focused on who might be the best to help him get the ranch into shape.

By the time he left the café, he had the names of five men looking for work, had promised that sometime soon he and Lana would have dinner with Angie and Harmon, and had been gifted a freshly baked, still warm apple pie.

He headed for home, the darkness of night making him think of Lana's sweet perfume, the silky sensation of her skin against his, the soft sighs she had emitted as he'd touched her here, there.

Heat filled him, the heat of desire, and he consciously tried to will it away. He didn't want to want

Lana. She was a duty to fulfill, a bargain to execute. Nothing more. She would never be anything more.

Still, he had to admit it was nice to pull into a driveway and see the porch light burning, knowing the porch light was on for him. Somebody waiting just for him.

She was on the sofa, watching the television when he walked in, and instantly he felt sorry...sorry for leaving her alone all day long, sorry for taking off for town without even having the courtesy to invite her along. Now, he couldn't remember what had made him run, what had made him feel as if he needed to escape.

She jumped up off the sofa and faced him. "I was beginning to wonder if you were coming home at all." The moment the words left her lips, she frowned. "I'm sorry, that sounded rather like a haranguing wife, didn't it?"

Chance set the pie on the coffee table, then reached for her hands. "No, I'm sorry," he said and pulled her down to sit next to him on the sofa. "I've been acting like a complete and total ass." He released her hands, finding them far too soft, far too feminine and warm.

"It's all right. This whole thing is awkward. You're in a position you don't want to be in."

"No, it's not all right," he said. "I've been acting like..." He frowned, realizing he'd been acting like his father. The brooding silences, the lack of respect for her, all of it was far too familiar for Chance.

"Like?" Her dark eyes gazed at him curiously.

"Never mind. Let's just say I've been behaving badly and I apologize."

She smiled, that full, sweet smile that lit her from within. "Apology accepted." It was that simple with her, no grudge holding, no ill will suppressed. Apology offered and accepted.

"I've got a freshly baked apple pie from Angie at the café. What do you say we have a cup of coffee and a piece of it before turning in for the night?"

"Sounds good."

Together they went into the kitchen and as Lana made the coffee, Chance cut the pie and slid two still-warm pieces on plates.

"I've got a list of men to call tomorrow about coming to work for me," he said once they were seated at the table. "There are so many things around here I just can't do by myself."

"I could help," she offered. A piece of piecrust clung to her lower lip, and Chance had the over-whelming desire to lean forward and pluck it off with his tongue.

"I don't need your help," he said, then realized his voice had been more brusque than he intended. He offered a smile to take any sting away. "If you'll just keep up with the work in here, then we'll have this place ready to sell in no time."

Thankfully, she used her napkin and the teasing crumb disappeared. "You've never considered stay-ing here and ranching? I don't mean staying married to me," she hurriedly added. "But there was a time when you used to talk about being a rancher."

"A long time ago." He stared down at the last of

his pie. "While I was at the Colton ranch, surrounded by their love and support, I somehow got it into my head that everything was going to be all right, that I'd return here and my father would love me and we'd work this place together and the world would be right." He smiled with a touch of bitterness. "Foolish dreams of a foolish kid."

"Not foolish," Lana protested and reached out to cover his hand with hers. "Idealistic, perhaps. But just because you couldn't find any peace with your father here, doesn't mean you can't find peace here now that he's gone."

He shook his head and pulled his hand from hers. "Too many bad memories between these walls. Besides, I prefer the vagabond life." He stood and carried his plate and his cup to the sink. "I'm going to turn in."

She nodded. "I'll be there in just a few minutes."

He left the kitchen, oddly disturbed by their conversation. Yes, there had been a time when he'd wanted to be a rancher, when he'd dreamed of working his father's spread and sleeping in the same bed night after night.

But this house held nightmare memories for him. Here and there was physical evidence of his father's rages. There was a hole in the Sheetrock in the spare bedroom, where his father had knocked him halfway through the wall. The bathroom door lock was busted, broken when his father had followed him in there to give him the "beating he deserved."

Sarge had believed in corporal punishment and he'd believed in raising his son to be a man, not a sissy. The lessons he taught his son were usually painful, both physically and mentally.

No, Chance would never, could never stay here. He'd sell the place, take the money and run back to the life he'd built for himself.

Chance started into the bedroom, then hesitated just inside the door. Lana permeated the room, her scent surrounded him and her presence seemed to fill the room.

Her perfume and lotion bottles now nestled next to his cologne on the top of the dresser. A doily sat beneath the bedside lamp, adding a feminine touch to the room.

A fat candle was on her bedside stand, its vanilla scent faint yet quite appealing. For just a moment he envisioned the candle lit and Lana naked in the bed with him.

The candlelight would add gold tones to her skin. It would lightly caress her pretty features and pull a rich shine from her long, dark hair.

Her skin would be warm against him, her mouth hot and eager as it had been the night before.

He undressed and slid beneath the covers, wondering how in the hell he was going to spend the night smelling her, feeling her warmth, and not give in to the overwhelming desire to make love to her again.

Four

"Chance?"

"Yeah?"

Lana rolled over on her side and tried to discern his features in the darkness of the bedroom. They had been lying side-by-side for half an hour, but she'd known he wasn't sleeping by his breathing and by his restless tossing and turning.

And she had been unable to sleep as she'd waited for him to touch her, to lean over and kiss her. She felt as if she were about to explode from not knowing what to expect. "Are we going to…" She allowed her voice to trail off.

There was a long moment of silence, then she sensed rather than saw him turning to face her. "I thought maybe you wouldn't feel like it tonight. I thought maybe…you know…you might be sore."

She could hear the tinge of embarrassment in his voice and was grateful for the cover of darkness to hide her own embarrassment. "I am a little tender," she admitted.

"Get a good night's sleep, Lana. There's always tomorrow night." He rolled over once again and within minutes she realized he'd fallen asleep.

Lana was both disappointed and relieved that there would be no lovemaking that night. She had a feeling that if they attempted it, she would find it uncomfortable, yet she longed to have him kiss her again, hold her in his strong arms.

She fell asleep and dreamed of Chance's body pressed against hers, his warmth surrounding her. She awakened at dawn, shocked to find that in sleep her body and Chance's had found each other.

His arm was thrown across her stomach and one of his legs was entwined with hers. His breath was warm against the side of her neck and he lay on her hair, effectively trapping her against him.

She was trapped, but she was a willing prisoner. His skin was toast-warm against her, and his masculine scent filled her senses. This is the way married people sleep, she thought. They share not only the intimacy of making love, but also the pleasure of waking in each other's arms.

Closing her eyes, she hoped he didn't awaken for a while. She just wanted to lie here and indulge in the sweet experience of his nearness.

She must have fallen back asleep, for when she opened her eyes once again, she was alone in the bed. She got up, pulled her robe around her and went into the bathroom. She quickly washed up, brushed her hair into a neat bun, then headed for the kitchen.

He was seated at the table, the morning paper stretched out before him and a cup of coffee in hand. He looked up as she entered, an open, unguarded smile curving his lips. "Good morning," he said.

She returned his smile and wondered if he had any idea how handsome he looked. Nobody wore jeans and a T-shirt as well as Chance Reilly. "Good morning. You want some breakfast?" she asked.

He shook his head. "Just coffee for me. I've never been much of a breakfast eater."

She poured herself a cup of coffee and joined him at the table. His hair was still damp from a shower and she could smell the faint scent of minty soap and shaving cream. The scent, so masculine and so intrinsically his, caused a wistful yearning to take residence in the pit of her stomach.

"Did you sleep well?" He folded the paper and shoved it aside.

"Like a log." She took a sip of her coffee and felt her cheeks warm as his gaze lingered on her.

"Why do you do that with your hair?" he asked.

She reached up with one hand and self-consciously touched the neat bun. "Why do I do what?"

"Pull it all back like that."

She shrugged. "I don't know. Habit I guess. When I'm working I pull it back for convenience sake."

"I wish you'd wear it loose more often." He broke his gaze from hers and stood. "And now it's time for me to get to work."

"Do you want me to bring lunch out to you?" she asked.

"No, I'll come in around noon. I'll make my phone calls to hire some help after lunch." With these words, he left the house.

Lana finished her coffee, then went into the bathroom to shower and dress for the day. A half an hour later she stood before the dresser mirror in the bedroom and stared at her reflection. He liked her hair, and he wished she'd wear it loose more often.

It seemed a simple enough request, and when she left the bedroom, her hair was loose and falling freely down her back.

The morning passed quickly as Lana busied herself with household chores and planning the evening meal.

It was just after eleven when a knock fell on the front door. Lana answered and squealed in delight as she saw her younger sister with her precious Marissa in her arms.

"Maya! Come in," she said as she reached out to take her niece. A gleeful chortle issued from Marissa as she held out her arms to Lana.

Lana cuddled Marissa close and kissed her solidly on the forehead, then grinned at her sister. "Come on into the kitchen. I just made some fresh lemonade."

"I shouldn't even be speaking to you," Maya said as she followed Lana into the kitchen. Her dark eyes flashed as she plopped down in a chair at the table.

"What did I do?" Lana asked as she sat, with Marissa on her lap, across from her beautiful sister.

"Without a word to anyone, you got married!" Maya glared at her as if she'd committed a heinous crime. "Mama told me this morning and I couldn't believe it!"

A wave of guilt swept through Lana. She'd specifically asked her mother not to tell Maya the real circumstances of her marriage to Chance.

Maya, flush with her love for her husband, Drake, would have never, ever understood the forces that had driven Lana into a loveless marriage with an expiration date.

"It all happened so fast," Lana said. She kissed the top of Marissa's head, loving the sweet scent of baby that clung to the little girl. "And if I remember correctly, I could be mad at you for the very same reasons. I don't recall attending your wedding and you didn't call me the moment this sweet baby arrived into the world." She smiled at her sister. "How about I pour us some lemonade and we forgive each other."

Maya leaned forward and reached for Lana's hand. "You know I can't stay mad at you. I just wish you would have given me an opportunity to be part of it. I could have thrown you a bridal shower, bought you a tacky gift, helped you shop for a wedding dress." She released Lana's hand and stood. "And I'll pour the lemonade so you get more quality time with the baby."

"Fine with me," Lana said and once again cuddled the dear little girl close. "She's getting so big," Lana exclaimed.

"They grow fast, don't they," Maya agreed. "We're hoping that before too long she'll have a little brother or a sister."

"And maybe a cousin," Lana added, her heart swelling at the very idea.

Maya clapped her hands together. "Wouldn't that be wonderful!"

The back door opened and Chance walked in.

"Ah, there he is," Maya said. "The man of the hour—my new brother-in-law." She reached up and gave Chance a smacking peck on the cheek. "Welcome to the fold."

"Thanks." He hugged her briefly, his gaze focused on Lana. "And that must be the amazing Marissa," he said.

"Indeed, it is!" Lana lifted the little girl up in the air, laughing as Marissa kicked her feet and waved her hands with excitement. "Isn't she just about the prettiest little girl you've ever seen in your life?"

Chance winked at Maya. "I can remember another little girl I thought was quite pretty."

Lana blushed as she realized he was talking about her. Of course, she knew he was just keeping up the pretense, but still, his words shot heat through her. She once again cradled the squirming, wiggling baby in her lap and began a game of pat-a-cake.

"I was just pouring us a glass of lemonade," Maya said. "You joining us?"

"Sounds good." He sat next to Lana at the table and Marissa stared at him solemnly, apparently measuring him to see if he was worthy of one of her drooling, toothless grins. He passed her test and she grinned at him, batting dark lashes flirtatiously.

"She's going to be a real heartbreaker," he said, a softness on his face Lana had never seen before.

Maya set the glasses of lemonade on the table, then sat down once again. She looked from Chance to Lana, then laughed. "I suppose I shouldn't be surprised that you two finally got together. Lana has never been as crazy about a guy as she was over you, Chance."

"Maya," Lana protested and shot her sister a look she hoped would make her change the subject, but Maya merely laughed.

"Oh, goodness, don't tell me Chance didn't know that you were absolutely besotted with him when you were a kid."

"Actually, I didn't know that," Chance said and once again looked at Lana, one of his golden-brown eyebrows lifted with amused interest.

"Everyone else knew it," Maya exclaimed, studiously ignoring Lana's pointed glare. "She drove us all crazy that year you lived with the Coltons. Even Meredith told me she wondered if Lana could complete a sentence without your name in it."

"She did not," Lana protested. "You're making that up."

"Maybe I am," Maya laughed, then sobered suddenly. "Of course, Meredith doesn't say much of anything nice to anyone anymore."

"What's going on with Meredith?" Chance asked.

Although Lana was grateful for the change of topic, thoughts of Meredith Colton always produced a deep sadness in her. "Meredith has changed, Chance."

"Changed how?" he asked, and she knew he was remembering the beautiful woman with the warm brown eyes and open smile who had welcomed him into their home.

"She's become a raving lunatic," Maya said. "She's mean-spirited and hateful and snaps at everyone who gets near her. If Mama and Dad didn't love Joe and the rest of the family so much, they probably would have quit working there by now."

Chance leaned back in his chair, obviously stunned by the news. "What happened to her? I mean, the person you just described is totally at odds with the woman I knew."

"The big change in her took place right after she had a terrible car accident," Lana said. "It was about ten years ago, not long after you left Prosperino. She and Emily were going somewhere and they crashed. Neither of them were seriously hurt, but I heard that Emily had horrible nightmares after that and Meredith was never the same."

"What about Joe? How's he doing?" Chance asked.

Again a wave of sadness shot through Lana. "Mama says he's just a shell, going through the motions, but most of the time he just seems lost."

Marissa laughed and clapped her hands together, as if to break the somber mood.

"I'd better get moving," Maya said with a glance at her watch. "I've got several more errands to run before this kid is ready for lunch."

"You sure you can't stay any longer?" Lana asked, reluctant to relinquish the baby girl in her arms. There was nothing quite as wonderful as holding a baby.

"Not today. But now that you're an old married

lady like me, we'll have to get together for lunch, exchange recipes and gossip,'' Maya said.

Lana nodded and gave Marissa one last kiss. ''Goodbye, sweet baby,'' she said softly. She looked up to see Chance staring at her, an odd expression on his face.

''You don't have to walk me out.'' Maya took Marissa from Lana's lap. ''See you two later.'' She gave a cheery wave, then walked out of the kitchen. A moment later the sound of the front door opening and closing indicated she was gone.

''You ready for some lunch?'' Lana asked, fidgeting nervously beneath Chance's steady gaze.

''No thanks,'' he said.

''You aren't hungry?''

''Actually, I am hungry…but I'm not hungry for lunch.''

It was a good thing Lana was sitting, for had she not been, her knees would have surely weakened by the sudden realization of what he was talking about.

Green flames lit his eyes, and even though she had never seen a man look at her in that way, there was a primal part of her that recognized it and responded.

''Then what are you hungry for?'' she asked, her voice half-breathless with anticipation and nerves. Her mouth was unbelievably dry.

He leaned forward and wrapped a strand of her hair slowly around his hand, pulling her forward with a gentle pressure. ''I'm hungry for the taste of your mouth, for the feel of your skin against mine.''

His words evoked a heat inside her, and his eyes

were like the sea, so green, so compelling. She wanted to fall into them, fall into him.

"Are you feeling better today?" he asked, his lips mere inches from hers.

"I'm feeling fine," she whispered, then blushed. "But, Chance…it's the middle of the day."

"We'll pull the drapes." He gave her no opportunity to protest, but instead stood and pulled her up and into his arms.

His mouth took possession of hers, his tongue seeking entry as his hands pressed her intimately against him. The sweet rush of wild sensations that had claimed her on the first night he'd kissed her returned, sending her senses reeling.

When he finally removed his mouth from hers, she was utterly breathless. He held out his hand to her and she took it, allowing him to lead her down the hallway and into their bedroom.

Once there, she stood and watched, her heart thudding in anticipation as he drew the heavy draperies across the windows, throwing the room into semi-darkness. He reached into the nightstand drawer and removed a package of matches, then lit the candle she had sitting on the top of the nightstand.

When he looked at her once again, his eyes reflected the glow of the candle. Lana's mouth grew dry once again and every nerve ending in her body felt as if it were on fire.

His gaze still locked with hers, he unbuttoned his shirt and shrugged it from his shoulders, letting it fall to the floor just behind him. The candlelight loved his chest, turning the springy hair into sparkles and sharply defining the muscles and planes.

He remained standing, watching her expectantly, and Lana suddenly realized what he wanted. Her fingers trembled as she raised her hands to the top button of her blouse. Never before had she felt the kind of raw, sexual want that she did at the moment. It was both exhilarating and more than a little bit frightening.

With the unclasping of each button, she was more exposed, but it was the flames in his eyes that urged her onward, until all the buttons were unfastened and she slid the blouse off her shoulders as he had done with his shirt.

His eyes flared as his gaze traveled across her lace-clad breasts. In three strides he had her once again in his arms, his mouth covering hers in a demanding kiss. At the same time his hands tangled in her hair.

When his lips finally left hers, he tugged gently on her hair and her head fell backward, giving his lips a trail to blaze down the length of her throat.

Conscious thought was impossible as his hands moved from the tangle of her hair to cover her breasts. Her nipples hardened, as if seeking the heat his hands offered.

"You are so beautiful," he murmured against her neck.

She wanted to tell him that he was beautiful, that she'd never seen a man quite so beautiful, but speaking was just as impossible as rational thought. She could only feel...feel Chance's body against hers, feel marvelous sensations and a depth of emotion.

Her breath caught in her throat as his hands left her breasts and instead touched the fastening of her jeans. With a simple flick of his fingers, the jeans were unfastened and his fingers moved the zipper down.

He stepped back from her only long enough for her to kick the jeans off altogether, then she reached for his waistband. As she undid his jeans, she could feel his desire pressing hard against her hand and her heart accelerated its pace.

He tore off his jeans and briefs, and at the same time Lana took off her bra and panties, wanting, needing to be naked with him, to feel his body against hers.

They fell to the bed, mouths locked and hands clutching, caressing, stroking the flames of desire higher and higher. She cried out as Chance explored one of her breasts with his mouth and swirled his tongue lightly across the peak.

She tangled her fingers in his hair as pressure built within her, a pressure she'd never felt before. She could feel it taking over her body, a need so incredible, a want so exquisite.

As his hands moved down the length of her, touching her with more intimacy than she'd ever allowed, the pressure intensified. She felt as if she were going to explode. She needed…needed something, but she wasn't sure what.

"Chance, I need you." Was that her voice, so breathless, so utterly wanton?

"Not yet, sweetheart," he whispered against her mouth as his fingers continued to dance at the core of her, building the tension until she thought she might explode.

Just when she thought she might scream, a wave of sensation swept through her, carrying her over a cliff and sending tiny shudders of bliss through her.

She clung to him, crying his name over and over again as the maelstrom of pleasure washed over her. Before she had time to recover, he moved between her thighs and entered her.

She tensed, expecting pain. But there was no pain, only a rebirth of a storm building within her. He took her slowly, riding the waves of desire with her.

Her hips moved of their own accord, arching up to meet his thrusts at the same time his mouth claimed hers in fiery want.

When he ended the kiss, his gaze bore into hers. Green seas, hypnotic and beautiful, beckoned her to fall in and drown. She cried out once again as the waves overtook her, pulling her under in a vortex of pleasure. At the same time she felt him stiffen against her, her name a hoarse cry on his lips.

For a long moment they remained entwined, their heartbeats slowing to a more normal pace, their bodies cooling without the heat of passion to warm them.

Now Lana understood what lovemaking was supposed to be. She'd never dreamed it would be so wonderful, so exciting, so…beautiful. Her body still tingled with the residual warmth of what they'd shared, and for just a moment, as their gazes had locked like their bodies were locked, she'd felt their connection had been more than physical.

He looked at her now, the flames gone from his

eyes, but still a tenderness remaining. "Are you okay?"

"I think so." She laughed suddenly. "My goodness, Chance, I never dreamed it would be so...so good."

He grinned, an open, wonderful grin that reminded her of the Chance of her childhood. "You mean even when you were young and thought you were madly in love with me, your fantasies didn't overrate me as a lover?"

"My fantasies were so innocent, I never got further than a kiss." She smiled teasingly. "But you kissed very well in those flights of fancy."

"Naturally," he replied, looking devilishly handsome and boyish with his hair all tousled. "And what about in reality?"

"Let's just say my fantasies didn't begin to live up to the reality."

He touched the tip of her nose with an index finger. "You were always a sweet kid and you've grown into a sweet woman." He rolled away from her and onto his back and stared at the ceiling thoughtfully. "That year I spent at the Coltons' place was the best year of my life."

Lana raised up on one elbow, loving the sight of him with the candle glow painting his body. She would be perfectly satisfied to lie here and look at him for hours. "It's been a long time since you've seen Meredith and Joe, hasn't it?"

He nodded. "Years. Whenever I came back here, I only stayed until I couldn't stand being around my dad any longer." He frowned. "Usually by the end of the first day, I was ready to hightail it out of here. There never seemed to be enough time to visit with anyone else.''

''Why don't you go over there and see them now?''

His frown deepened. ''After listening to you and Maya talking about Meredith, I don't want to see her. I'd rather remember them like they were.''

A bitter laugh escaped him and he sat up. ''Hearing the way Meredith and Joe have fallen apart merely proves what I've always believed.''

''And what's that?'' she asked softly.

His eyes glittered with a harsh light. ''That there is no such thing as lasting love, and anyone who believes otherwise is just a fool.''

''Surely you don't really believe that,'' she protested softly. ''What about my parents? They are as in love with each other today as the day they married years ago.''

''They are the exception, not the rule. And even if I did believe in love and marriage, I know it isn't for me.'' He rolled off the bed and grabbed his jeans and quickly pulled them on. ''I've got to get back to work.''

Lana sat up and grabbed the blanket around her, suddenly feeling cold and naked. ''What about lunch?''

''I'm not hungry.'' He picked up his shirt and headed out the door.

She pulled the blanket more firmly around her. How quickly he transformed from passionate and tender to hurting and defensive. His actions and words served to remind her that she couldn't fall into any fantasy where he was concerned.

It would be easy, with the flush of their lovemaking still on her skin, with the residual heat of his touch still coursing through her, to believe that they might have a future together. It would be so easy to lose herself in the softness she'd seen momentarily in his eyes, and to believe that he might fall in love with her.

But to do so would be utter foolishness. She absolutely, positively could not allow herself to forget for one minute that this marriage was nothing more than a temporary arrangement.

Jackson, Mississippi. Meredith Colton stared out the window onto the city where she had been living, as if by looking at the scenery she could somehow reclaim the memory of all the events that had brought her here years before.

Some of her memories were still obscured by the darkness of amnesia, others had become crystal-clear, leaving her in a sort of shadowy transitional place between living her own life and somebody else's.

She stepped away from the window and instead walked over to the desk. She picked up the nameplate that read Dr. Martha Wilkes, and ran her fingers lightly over the etched golden letters.

Had it not been for Dr. Wilkes, Meredith still might be living her life believing she was her twin sister, Patsy Portman. Now she knew the truth, that ten years ago her sister had run her car off the road and in the aftermath of that accident Patsy had stolen Meredith's

life, leaving Meredith to ten years of amnesia, nightmares and unanswered questions about herself.

"I'm sorry to keep you waiting." Dr. Wilkes swept
into the room, an apologetic smile on her beautiful
ebony face.

"I didn't mind waiting." Meredith set the nameplate back on the desk, then took a seat on the settee
that faced the desk.

Dr. Wilkes joined her there rather than taking a seat
behind her desk. "How are you feeling?" Her dark
eyes radiated not only curiosity but also an empathy
that Meredith found comforting.

She frowned. "Excited…afraid…confused. Memories are coming faster and faster now, but there are
still so many holes."

Dr. Wilkes nodded. "You've learned a lot about
yourself in the last couple of weeks. The surprise visit
from Rand and Emily opened up the floodgates of
your memory."

Meredith smiled at thoughts of her oldest son and
her sweet, adopted daughter Emily. At first, Meredith
hadn't recognized either of them, but as they talked
to her, told her what they'd managed to piece together
about the day of the car accident and the intervening
years with Patsy acting as Meredith, Meredith's memories had begun to emerge from the dark place where
they had been hiding.

Her first, strong memory had grown out of the
nightmare she'd suffered for the past ten years. It was
the nightmare of a little red-haired girl crying out to
her. "Mommy, where are you? Help me. Please, help
me," the child in her dreams had cried.

Meredith would awaken crying because she knew the child needed her, but she couldn't remember who the child was. A grief almost too intense to bear would ache in her heart for days after one of those nightmares.

Now the little girl had a name and the memories to go with the name. Sweet Emily. Meredith's adopted daughter.

"I'm sad, too," Meredith said, although *sad* was too weak a word to describe what was in her heart. "My little sparrow Emily isn't little anymore."

Instead of the little red-haired girl of her nightmares, Emily was now twenty years old with a mane of chestnut-red hair that framed her beautiful face. "I've missed so much—ten years…a decade…a lifetime. And what I keep wondering is what has Patsy managed to destroy in those years."

"You're talking about your relationship with Joe," Dr. Wilkes said.

Meredith nodded. Joe Colton. Her husband. Memories of him were still fuzzy. Until Rand and Emily's visit to her, she hadn't even known his name.

What had survived through the amnesia was the memory of strong arms holding her, of a special man who had been her other half, her soul mate. He'd had no name, no face, but she'd had the memory of their love in her heart.

Dr. Wilkes leaned forward and took Meredith's hand in hers. "I can't allay that fear for you, Meredith. When you decide that it's time to go home and reclaim your life from your sister, you know there will be a period of adjustment for you and your family. There will be a lot of pieces to pick up." She released Meredith's hand.

Meredith only hoped the pieces of her life and her family could be picked up. "There's one other thing," Meredith said as she nervously twisted her hands together in her lap.

"And what's that?"

"I have a terrible sense of impending doom, of imminent danger. It's a feeling I've only had once before in my life."

"When was the last time you felt this way?" Dr. Wilkes asked, leaning forward.

Meredith drew a shaky breath. "The day I got in the car with Emily, the day we had our accident. I felt this way the morning of the day that my twin sister stole my identity and completely destroyed my life."

Five

———

Chance stood by the corral, watching as a load of lumber was dumped nearby. He waved to the driver who created a cloud of dust as he drove away.

"Guess that means it's time to get back to work," Kirk Brighton said, rising from the bale of hay where he'd been sitting. The other three men Chance had hired the week before also got up from their various positions of rest.

They'd spent the last week cleaning out the barn, repairing any woodwork that needed repairing, then putting on a new coat of paint. Despite the pleasant September air, the work had been hot and dirty.

That morning they had torn down the corral in anticipation of putting up a new one. Although there was no longer any livestock on the Reilly ranch,

Chance knew whoever bought the place would need adequate corrals and fencing for horses or cows.

Much to his surprise, Chance had enjoyed the physical labor the last week had brought. Working as a traveling salesman, the most physical thing he'd accomplished was an occasional swim in a motel pool or a quick workout in a gym facility.

For Chance, the most satisfying time of the day was those minutes after the men knocked off for the day and before Chance went inside for dinner. He'd walk in the waning sunlight, muscles burning with the sting of overuse, as he looked at the work they'd accomplished that day.

He frowned as he recognized this wasn't exactly true. That moment in the fade of day wasn't the most satisfying. It was in the deep velvet black of night when he reached for Lana and she came willingly into his arms that Chance felt something he'd never felt before—a surge of excitement so intense it threatened to consume him, followed by a sense of fulfillment that absolutely terrified him.

They came together each night with a fierce intensity that was in direct opposition to the careful distance they kept between them during the day.

"Hey, Chance."

Chance shoved away thoughts of Lana and focused his attention on Charlie Trainor, the eldest of the four men he'd hired. "Yeah, Charlie?"

"When you get ready to buy a herd of cattle, I've got just the man for you to talk to," he said.

Chance didn't want to tell anyone that he had no intentions of settling on the place, that he intended to sell it as soon as it was in good order. He didn't want to have to handle the kinds of questions people would ask if they knew he wasn't staying.

Everyone would want to know where he and Lana were moving to and he didn't want to have to explain that he and Lana were going nowhere together. He would go back to his wandering lifestyle, and she would return to her apartment and have a baby to raise.

"Thanks, Charlie. I'll keep that in mind when the time comes and I'm ready to buy."

"You talking about old man Stanton?" Kirk Brighton asked Charlie.

Charlie nodded. "That bull of Stanton's is a fine specimen of cowhide and he's got a herd of healthy heifers that make most other ranchers' cows look sick."

As the men worked on the new corral, they talked about ranching, filling Chance in on who had the better horses and where to buy the best feed. It didn't take long for the conversation to turn to other things—the bar that had the best drinks in town, favorite baseball teams and the new motor that some guy named Dirk had dropped into his old Chevy.

Chance was surprised to discover himself enjoying the male conversation. One of the negatives of always traveling was the lack of any real companionship.

Even as a young man, Chance had been reluctant to form any real or lasting friendships with other guys. Friends spent time at your house, and Chance had never wanted to expose anyone to his volatile father.

The aura of camaraderie that now surrounded him reminded him of his happy days on the Colton ranch. For that year of his life he'd felt a part of something bigger than himself. He'd been part of a community, a family.

He frowned, remembering what Maya and Lana had said about Meredith Colton. It shouldn't surprise him. He'd always believed in his heart that good things didn't last, that happiness wasn't forever.

He'd had a brief period of happiness when his mother had been alive, but when she'd died, she'd taken everything good in his life with her. And Meredith Colton had turned into a mean, hateful woman. Good things didn't last.

They'd been working on the corral for about two hours when Chance saw Lana approach from the house. Clad in a bright pink dress and with her hair streaming like a curtain of silk down her back, she carried a huge pitcher and several large paper cups.

Chance had never before noticed how sensually her hips undulated when she walked and how her silky curtain of hair swayed in tantalizing rhythm.

The press of her breasts were evident against the dress bodice and Chance's hands itched with a sudden need to touch her.

He knew he'd awakened in her a well of passion, and he found her an intriguing and exciting bundle of shyness and boldness in bed.

A strange thrill of possession swept through him along with an unexpected pride as he watched the other ranch hands stand and eye her approach with obvious approval.

"I thought you all might like something cold to drink," she said, that familiar shy smile lighting her features.

"That sounds mighty good, ma'am," Clayton Croft, the youngest of the group, said as he quickly swept his hat from his head.

Chance had the feeling that if Lana had offered to serve hot beer to the young man, he'd have jumped at the opportunity to please her.

"Oh, please, I'm not a ma'am, I'm just Lana," she said as she poured the young cowboy a tall glass of lemonade.

"Thank you, ma'am, uh, Lana." Clayton took the cup from her, the color in his cheeks heightening as he offered her a shy smile. Clayton watched her every move with mooning eyes, and amusement filled Chance.

She poured the cold drink for the others, then started back to the house. Chance quickly fell in step with her. "That was a real thoughtful thing to do," he said.

She smiled at him and shrugged. "It's hot and dusty. I figured you could all use something cold to drink."

They stopped walking at the porch. "I think you made a conquest." Chance shot an amused glance toward Clayton.

"Don't be silly. I didn't do anything," she protested with a laugh.

Chance eyed her objectively and realized there was something different about her, a subtle something that hadn't been there on the day he'd married her.

An awareness of herself as a woman, a pride in the tilt of her head, a knowing gleam that lit her dark eyes. She was a woman who was desired...and knew it.

"How would you like to go out to dinner this evening?" he asked, suddenly wanting to go into town, let the people of Prosperino see his wife on his arm.

"Really?" she asked. "But I have a ham in the oven."

"Take it out and put it in the refrigerator. We'll eat it tomorrow night," he said firmly. "We haven't left this ranch together since our wedding day and it's high time I take my wife out for a meal."

She smiled up at him, her beautiful eyes lit with sparks of pleasure. "Oh, Chance, I'd like that."

Chance looked at his watch. "It's almost four now. I'll knock off work about five and we'll head out of here at six, okay?"

"I'll be ready." She turned and lightly ran up the steps to the door.

Chance watched until she disappeared into the house, then he walked back to the men.

"You're one lucky man, Chance Reilly," Charlie said. "That's a real pretty wife you've got, and she comes from good stock. You won't find better people than Inez and Marco Ramirez."

Chance nodded and together the men got back to work. *You're a lucky man.* As Chance hammered nails and carried wood, Charlie's words played and replayed in his mind.

Yeah, he was lucky all right. He had a wife who cleaned his house, cooked him sumptuous meals,

washed and ironed his clothes and met him with passion each night. And he didn't have to pretend to love
her or worry about promises of forever.

In the next couple of months he had every intention
of walking away from her. He should be happy about
it. He was living every single man's dream. But, as
Charlie's words continued to echo in his head, he
didn't feel particularly happy. He felt as if he just
might be more than a little bit stupid.

"It's high time I take my wife out for a meal."

Chance's words swirled in Lana's head as she
changed her clothes and prepared for an evening out
on the town. She wasn't sure why, but the thought of
going out to dinner with Chance filled her with nervous anxiety.

It somehow made the marriage seem more real than
it was, and Lana knew she couldn't fall into the fantasy of believing this was anything but a temporary
business arrangement.

Even though she knew Chance liked making love
to her, that didn't mean he loved her. She'd been a
virgin, but she certainly had listened to enough girl
talk to know that men were able to separate love and
sex quite easily.

She frowned at her reflection, wondering if perhaps
she'd overdone it with the makeup. She rarely wore
it, but had wanted to look nice, to look special for
their night out.

She pulled a tissue from the box and quickly
swiped it over her cheeks to take off some of the

blush she'd just applied. Checking her reflection, she pronounced herself ready.

The dress she'd chosen was nicer than her daily wear things. The scarlet dress hugged her figure to the waist, then flared out in a skirt that showed off her long legs. She'd used the curling iron on her hair, giving the length a touch of curl at the ends. She sprayed on a final spritz of her perfume, then left the bedroom.

As she walked down the hall, she heard Chance dressing in the bathroom. It was funny, they shared a bed every night. Three times that week he'd made love to her by candlelight, allowing her to see every inch of his body and him to view hers, yet when they dressed, he went into the bathroom and left her the privacy of the bedroom.

Once in the living room, she sat on the sofa and tried to still her nerves. It was ridiculous to be so anxious about a simple dinner out. They would eat, visit with people they knew, pretend to be happy in their marriage, then come home and return to their life for the time being.

She rubbed a hand across her abdomen, wondering if it had already happened. Had they already made a baby? Her heart thrilled at the very idea of carrying a tiny life inside her. At the same time, she hoped it didn't happen too soon. Once she was pregnant, there would be no more reason for Chance to kiss her, to hold her, to make love to her.

"Wow!"

She looked up to see Chance standing at the end of the hallway, his gaze focused intently on her. He was dressed in a pair of charcoal-gray slacks and a striped dress shirt, but she suddenly feared she'd over-dressed. Perhaps he had meant a simple meal at the café. She stood and ran her hands down the sides of her skirt. "Too much?" she asked worriedly.

"No, not at all." He approached her, his intense gaze sweeping over her, taking her in from head to toe. Her body warmed at every point where his gaze lingered. "It's just that you look...you look beautiful."

Heat rose to her cheeks, a sweet heat of pleasure. "Thank you." She averted her gaze from his, afraid that if she continued to look into the flames in his green eyes, she'd fall right into him and they'd never make it to dinner. "Are you ready?" she asked softly.

"Oh, sweetheart, you have no idea how ready I am."

The fire in her cheeks intensified. "I was talking about going to dinner," she said dryly.

He swept a finger across her lower lip, the touch achingly sensual. "Okay, but after dinner, when we get back here, I intend to take you where I'm ready to go."

As they left the house and got into his car, Lana wondered how it was possible he could make her feel so breathless, so wonderfully alive. A simple touch, a certain look in his eyes, and she was weak-kneed and dizzy with burning want.

Was it this way with all couples? Somehow, she didn't think so. There was a strong physical attraction at work between Chance and her, but she'd be a fool to mistake it for anything more. She'd be a fool to mistake it for love.

Still, as he drove toward town, she basked in his nearness. Despite their lovemaking, they rarely spent any real time together. They shared the evening meal, but most evenings Chance was tired and withdrawn and any conversation between them was strained and uncomfortable.

She sensed something different in Chance tonight. He seemed invigorated rather than drained from the day's work. As music from the radio filled the car, his thumbs thumped in rhythm on the steering wheel and he hummed beneath his breath.

Perhaps he was invigorated by the idea of getting off the ranch he professed to hate. Maybe it was the idea of being surrounded by people and not just in her company that had him in high spirits.

"You and the men are getting a lot accomplished in a short amount of time," she said to break the silence between them.

He turned the radio down just a touch. "They're a good bunch of workers. We should finish up the corral this week and then next week start on some of the pasture fencing."

"I made a list of things you might want to think about fixing in the house," she said. He looked at her in surprise and she smiled. "You've been focused in on fixing all the things that will make a man want to buy the ranch, but the real person you need to please is a buyer's wife."

"You think so?" he asked, obviously intrigued by the idea.

"I'm certain. With that in mind, I walked through each room this morning and pretended to be a prospective buyer looking at the place as if it was going to be my home for the next fifty years or so." What she didn't tell him was that it was far too easy for her to imagine living there for the next fifty years...with him.

"And what did you find?" he asked.

"The leaky faucet in the kitchen needs to be replaced. The bathroom door lock is broken. One burner on the stove doesn't work, and there's a dent in the Sheetrock in the spare room." She ticked off the items one after another, and felt a sudden tension rolling off Chance. "What?" She frowned worriedly. "What did I say that's upset you?"

He cast her a swift look of surprise. "What makes you think you've upset me?"

She shrugged. "I can feel it. Besides, you're suddenly grabbing the steering wheel too tightly and your jaw is clenched."

His fingers loosened around the wheel and he released a deep sigh. "I'll fix the faucet and we'll buy a new burner for the stove, but I won't replace the Sheetrock or the bathroom door lock."

It was her turn to look at him in surprise. "Why not?"

He frowned, his features looking hard in the glow from the dashboard lights. "I won't clean up his messes. Faucets and burners wear out, but door locks and Sheetrock get broken through violence."

Lana felt the pain beneath the anger in his voice. "I'm sorry, Chance." She reached out and placed a hand on his thigh in an effort to comfort. "I'm sorry you didn't have a father like mine, one who would support you and love you, one who never raised his voice or his fists in anger."

He dropped a hand from the steering wheel and covered hers with it. "I always envied you your relationship with your parents. And for that year that I lived on the Colton ranch, I tried to pretend I wasn't Chance Reilly, but instead was Chance Colton."

"I was lucky by birth," she said softly, warmed by the touch of his hand against hers. "You'll just have to find happiness and be lucky in the choices you make and the direction you choose for your life." She turned her hand over so her fingers could entwine with his. "Maybe in fixing the wall and the lock, you'll heal some of the pain, get rid of some of the anger inside you."

He pulled his hand away and returned it to the steering wheel. "I've got no pain inside me, and the anger will go away when I sell that place and spend his money for my pleasure."

He might think he had no pain from his childhood, but Lana knew otherwise and she wondered if he was spending his life running from his pain, the end result a lifestyle of no ties and no commitments to anything and anyone.

"I didn't mean to place a pall on things," she finally said, then offered him a teasing smile. "After all, it isn't every night my husband takes me out to dinner."

"That's right," he agreed, returning her smile with one of his own. "But I do have a word of advice."

"What?"

"If you don't take your hand off my thigh, we'll never make it through dinner. I'll be wanting to carry you off to the nearest motel and have my way with you." His eyes glittered with a fiery glow.

She quickly pulled her hand away, a deep blush warming her cheeks. "If you don't stop looking at me that way, I'll let you carry me off to the nearest motel and have your way with me." Her blush deepened as she shocked herself with her own boldness. "And in a single week, you've made me utterly shameless," she admitted.

She sobered slightly, her gaze lingering on him. "Is it wrong, Chance, for me to like sex so much? Am I…abnormal?"

He laughed and she felt the tension that had been in the air dissipate. "No, my sweet, innocent Lana. It isn't wrong and it isn't abnormal. We're good together in bed. And it's okay for you to be shameless just as long as it's always with me."

Always. The word teased the tip of her tongue, but she knew better than to speak it aloud. He was teasing her, but she wasn't sure her answer would be in the same teasing tone. With every day that passed she was more confused about her feelings where Chance was concerned.

He wheeled into Medicino's, a popular Italian restaurant. "How does Italian sound?"

"Wonderful," she replied.

Within minutes they were seated at a table near the back of the place. The ambience in the restaurant promoted romance. Candles burned in the center of each small table and hanging plants provided an aura of privacy. The tables were set far enough apart to allow intimate conversations and the music that drifted lightly in the air was soft and slow.

They placed their orders, then Chance poured them each a glass of wine from the bottle he'd ordered. "Did I tell you that you look quite lovely tonight?"

"You mentioned it earlier," she replied. He'd told her by the look in his eyes that he thought she looked good, but it was nice to hear the actual sentiment put into words once again.

"Then I'll tell you again. You look beautiful."

"You must drive those midwestern women crazy with your sweet talk and handsome looks," she returned lightly. She'd bet he had a girlfriend in every city, a warm female in every motel bed where he slept. She was surprised by how much this idea bothered her. She'd never had a jealous bone in her body, but the thought of Chance with other women caused a slight edge of jealousy to surge up inside her.

"Ah, finally we see the newlyweds out together."

Lana and Chance looked up to see Angie and Harmon Graves approaching their table. Angie leaned down and kissed Lana on the cheek. "Congratulations, sweetie. I'm glad to see one of our hometown girls managed to grab this scalawag."

"Thanks, Angie," Lana replied, and fought down a dose of guilt at their deception.

"What are you two doing here?" Chance asked.

Harmon pointed a finger at his wife. "She's quit cooking at home, so when she gets a night off, we eat out."

"I cook all day for other people, on my nights off I want somebody else cooking what I put in my mouth," Angie exclaimed.

"I've been meaning to call you and thank you for that beautiful apple pie you sent home with Chance. I've always said you make the best apple pies in California and we really enjoyed it," Lana said.

"Don't mention it," Angie said with a pleased smile.

"Would you two like to join us?" Chance asked.

"Heavens no. You two are practically still on your honeymoon and we wouldn't dream of intruding," Angie exclaimed. "Enjoy your dinner," she said, then grabbed her husband's arm. "Come on, Harmon, I'm starving."

Harmon nodded goodbye in his usual laconic fashion and the two disappeared.

"Angie is a sweetheart," Lana said the moment they had left.

Chance nodded. "She and Harmon were my lifeline on more than one occasion."

"What do you mean?"

"When things got too tough between me and my dad and I needed an escape, I'd often go to the café and hang out there. Angie was always very sympathetic and Harmon…" Chance laughed. "Harmon never said much, but when he did speak, he usually said something important."

Lana took a sip of her wine, then leaned forward. "Tell me about your job, Chance. Tell me about your life in the Midwest."

It was odd really. She'd slept with him for a little

over a week now, but didn't feel as if she'd discovered all the pieces that made him who he was. Perhaps in hearing about how he spent his days, she'd learn more facets of the man.

"There isn't a whole lot to tell. I cover a five-state area and have regular customers I sell to, but I'm also always on the lookout for new accounts." He paused to sip his wine, then continued. "I spend a lot of time in my car, driving from one place to the next. Of course at the moment I've taken a leave of absence."

"You enjoy driving?" she asked.

He frowned thoughtfully. "Not particularly."

"But you like being in a different place every day?"

"Sure." The frown disappeared from his face and he leaned back in his chair. "I love seeing different faces and different places. I like the fact that I set my own schedule. I eat when I get hungry, sleep when I'm tired and owe nobody any explanation for anything. As long as I'm selling farm equipment, my boss is happy and stays off my back."

"But don't you get lonely?" She couldn't imagine the kind of life he had just described, rarely seeing the same people twice, waking in a different bed every morning. "It must be difficult to sustain any kind of friendships, any kind of meaningful relationships."

His eyes took on a hardness. "I sustain the kind of relationships that suit me best—sort of like this one with you. Temporary ones."

Again she felt as if she was being warned. Only this time, with the warning came a certain, dreadful realization. Years ago she had been able to fall out of love with Chance Reilly. But the stunning realization was that at some point in the last week, she'd fallen in love with him all over again.

Six

The discussion about his lifestyle had disturbed him. He'd thought he loved his life as a traveling salesman until she'd questioned him about it and forced him to examine it more closely.

The hours on the road, the mornings he'd awakened and not remembered what town he was in, the nights alone in a motel room all had been conducive to a loneliness he just now recognized.

And that realization had upset him and prompted him to snap at Lana and remind her that he intended to return to the life he'd lived before his father's death.

She'd been quiet since then and Chance found himself wanting to see her laugh, needing to see her eyes sparkle with pleasure and her lips curve into the smile he found so bewitching.

"Have I told you about the summer I tried to join the circus?" he asked.

Her beautiful dark eyes looked at him in surprise. "No."

"I was twelve and the circus had come to Prosperino." He finished the last of his wine, then continued. "By then I already knew how tough things were going to be between my father and me, so I decided a circus life seemed very appealing. But I knew I needed a special talent in order to be allowed to join the big top."

Lana leaned forward, the scent of her perfume reaching out to surround him as a smile of anticipation lit her features. "So, what did you do?"

"For weeks before the circus arrived here, I tried to come up with something, some gimmick. I tried juggling, but quickly learned that I wasn't quick or dexterous enough. So, I decided I'd learn how to swing on a trapeze."

Lana clapped a hand over her mouth, her eyes filled with laughter and Chance continued, wanting to keep the smile on her face. "I rigged up a couple of ropes and some wood in a big tree down in the pasture."

Her big brown eyes were the color of dark chocolates. "I'm assuming you weren't successful since you didn't leave when the circus did."

"The first time I swung on my homemade trapeze, the rope broke and I was thrown up in the air and landed on my back about ten feet from the tree. All the air left my body and for a moment I thought sure I was dead. When I finally was able to breathe I was too scared to try it again. So, I was a flop in my attempt to join the circus.''

The waitress appeared to take away their plates and they each ordered a cup of coffee. As they drank their coffee, their conversation remained pleasant. They spoke about their time together on the Colton ranch, speculated on what had changed Meredith Colton from a warm, generous woman to a spiteful, hateful witch.

Lana caught him up on the local gossip, telling him who had married and who had divorced. Chance enjoyed watching her as she spoke. Her expressive face reflected her thoughts and her words.

As they talked, several locals waved to Lana or greeted her with friendliness. It was easy for Chance to recognize that Lana was somebody well-liked and respected in the community.

He also found himself anticipating later that night, when they were in his bed and he could hold her warm body against his.

It was strange, he'd always thought making love to somebody new was a turn-on, that the novelty and discovery of an initial joining was the peak of excitement and repeating the experience with the same woman only became mundane.

He'd been wrong. Making love to Lana night after night had not become mundane or boring, rather his pleasure had been increased by learning and memorizing her sweet responses to his various touches. There was definitely something positive to say about familiarity.

Gazing at her, he noticed how the candlelight positively loved her, caressing her features with a golden softness and dancing like fireflies on the length of her hair.

When he'd first seen her in that dangerous red dress, he'd wanted to forget dinner, forget leaving the house and instead sweep her into the bedroom and tear the garment off her.

As they'd eaten their meal, he'd been aware of other men looking at her, coveting her with heated gazes and again he'd felt the same curious thrill of possession that he'd felt when he'd seen the young Clayton stammering and blushing.

These men could look all they wanted, but she was coming home with him. She would be in his bed, in his arms, kissing his mouth before the night was over.

"Are you ready to go?" he asked when he'd paid their bill and they'd finished their coffee.

She nodded, dabbed her lips with her napkin, then stood.

It was just after eight-thirty when they stepped out of the restaurant and onto the sidewalk. "You want to walk a little bit?" he asked, then grinned. "I definitely ate too much."

In truth, the anticipation of making love to her filled him up, but his stomach felt heavy from the meal. Besides, a little walk would merely serve to further whet his appetite for her.

"Me, too. A walk sounds good," she agreed.

They started off at a leisurely pace, and it only seemed natural that he reach out and grab her hand in his. He liked her hands. They were soft and delicately feminine. She had long fingers with short, but well-manicured nails. And he knew what those hands could do to him—stroke, caress, touch him with a heat that boiled his blood.

"This is my favorite time of the day," he said, noting the sun was well into its descent, giving the landscape a golden glow.

"Why now?" she asked.

"I don't know. This is about the time I take my final walk around the ranch, check the progress of our work and feel a nice sense of accomplishment over what we've done for the day. Dusk has always been the time I take a few minutes and reflect."

"My moments of reflection come just before I close my eyes to go to sleep," she explained. "I think about the day gone and the one I'll face when I open my eyes."

He smiled at her wryly. "I imagine since living with me, you fall asleep before you have time to reflect."

"Why do you say that?" she asked.

"You do so much during the days. The house is always clean, my clothes are always washed and smell wonderful, each night you cook a terrific meal. You've got to be exhausted when you fall into bed at night."

Her eyes twinkled with a slightly naughty glow. "But not too exhausted for other things."

Chance laughed, his blood heating to dangerous temperatures. "I've created a monster."

It was her turn to laugh, then she sobered and her cheeks pinkened slightly. "Seriously, I had no idea it would be this way.'' The blush on her cheeks intensified. "I had no idea I'd like it so much.''

"That's because I'm an exceptionally skilled and magnificent lover,'' Chance teased.

"I think you might be right,'' she replied and again Chance's inner temperature rose. "Oh, look,'' she said suddenly. "It finally opened.'' She pointed across the street to a shop that had a Grand Opening sign in the window. "I've been waiting and waiting for it to open up.''

"Then I guess we'd better go in and take a look around,'' Chance said.

Her eyes shone with excitement and she clapped her hands together. "You mean it? I mean, I could always come back another time by myself.''

Chance smiled at her with amused indulgence. "You just said you've been waiting and waiting. I don't want you to wait another minute. Just lead the way.''

She tugged on his hand and pulled him toward the corner where they could cross the street, as if afraid he might change his mind.

Chance figured it was some kind of a dress boutique or maybe one of those stores that sold sexy lingerie. It wasn't until she was pulling him over the threshold that he realized exactly what kind of store it was—a baby store.

Strollers, cribs, high chairs and bassinets were prominently displayed just inside the door. Farther in the back were racks of clothing, bottles, stuffed animals, apparently everything needed to make a healthy, happy baby.

Chance wanted to back out of the door, take Lana by the hand and escape from the sweet-smelling store with its pastel-colored walls and lullaby music. But Lana was already off and running, oohing and aahing over an oak crib with a canopy.

"Oh, Chance, isn't it beautiful?" she asked, her eyes shining with the same kind of glow they'd possessed when she had held her niece.

"You have great taste," a saleslady said as she approached where Chance and Lana stood. She placed a hand on the crib railing. "This is one of the top of the line with extra safety features and the added highlight that it changes into a toddler bed when the little one gets too big for a crib."

Lana smiled wistfully. "It is beautiful." She gazed at the price tag and winced. "We're just window shopping right now," she explained to the sales clerk.

"Please, feel free to wander around the store." She winked at Lana. "And if you fill out a card to get on our mailing list, we'll give you a free gift." She smiled with genuine friendliness. "The gift isn't so great, but the flyers will let you know when we're running special sales, and you never know when this crib might go on special."

"Thanks, I'll fill out a card," Lana said.

"I'll just leave you two to wander." The woman drifted away to greet another couple entering the shop.

Reluctantly Chance followed behind Lana as she went up and down the aisles, lingering over itty-bitty sleepers, soft receiving blankets and amusing tiny

T-shirts. He couldn't help but grin as she held up a pair of the smallest cowboy boots he'd ever seen.

Still, as he watched her running her fingers over the soft blankets, it was easy to imagine her with a baby in her arms.

She would be an excellent mother, strong enough to raise a child with patience and love. Her child would be one of the lucky ones—desperately wanted and loved. Her little boy or girl would never know the sting of demeaning words, would never know the pain of a backhand or fist in the face.

My child.

The words suddenly shouted in his head. The baby she would carry would not just be hers but his as well. Half of his DNA would be carried by the baby Lana eventually had.

Although on some level, he'd known this, he hadn't truly thought about it until this very moment. Genetically, he would always be bound to her child. What would she tell her child about its father? That the child had been created so Daddy could get his ranch and leave forever? He suddenly needed to know how she was going to handle telling a little boy or a little girl about him.

"Lana?"

"Hmm," she said absently, her attention focused on a night-light that also played music.

"What are you going to tell the baby about me?"

That got her undivided attention. She looked at him in surprise. "I'm not sure...I hadn't really thought about it."

"Sooner or later a baby grows up and has questions

that need to be answered." Chance frowned. "Are you going to tell him or her about our bargain?"

Lana mirrored his frown thoughtfully. "No," she finally said decisively. "I'll just say that we married, it didn't work out and we divorced. In this day and age, divorce is so common."

"And what if he asks why I'm not a part of his life?"

Her frown deepened. "I don't know, Chance. I can't tell you right now exactly what I'm going to say. But, whatever I say, it will be in the best interest of the child."

Chance nodded, satisfied with her answer for the moment.

He was relieved when she finally started for the door, stopping only at the counter to fill out a card to be placed on the mailing list. He watched over her shoulder as she filled it out, somehow disquieted when he saw her write the address to her apartment rather than the ranch.

"You could have written down the ranch address," he said to her as they left the shop and headed back to his car.

She shrugged. "There's really no point. I check my mail at my apartment every week or so, and we'll be divorced and you'll be gone from Prosperino long before the baby is born."

Although he knew she was right, and it had been what he'd been reminding her of from the moment they'd gotten married, he couldn't understand why her cool, unemotional recitation of the facts somehow depressed him.

* * *

"So, how does it feel to be celebrating your one-month anniversary?" Maya asked her sister. "Do you and Chance have anything special planned for the night?"

"No, nothing." Lana speared a tomato from her salad, but instead of eating it, set her fork down across the side of her plate. "Maya, I have a confession to make."

The two were seated in Chance's kitchen. Rain had cancelled any work for the day and Chance had driven into town to order more supplies and eat lunch with an old friend from high school. He'd told her he'd be home in time for dinner.

Lana had taken the opportunity to invite her sister over for lunch with the express purpose of confessing the real reasons behind her marriage to Chance.

"A confession? Hmm, sounds intriguing." Maya shot a glance at her daughter, sleeping soundly in an infant carrier on the floor, then gazed once again at her sister.

Lana took a deep breath, dreading telling her sister the truth, yet unable to continue the charade. "My marriage to Chance isn't real."

Maya frowned in confusion. "What do you mean, it isn't real? You didn't really get married by a justice of the peace?" A grin curved the corners of her lips and her eyes widened. "Are you telling me that my proper, straitlaced older sister is living in sin with a man?"

"No, it's nothing like that," Lana hurriedly protested. "We really got married, but we have no intention of staying married."

"What?" Maya leaned forward, any hint of a smile gone.

Lana stared down at her salad and prepared herself for her sister's reaction to what she was about to say. "It was a business arrangement. Chance couldn't inherit this place unless he was married. His father had it written in his will that way." She glanced back up to see Maya staring at her in shock.

"You married Chance so he could inherit the ranch?" Her voice held a note of incredulity. "And what do you get out of this—this business arrangement?"

"A baby."

Maya gasped. "Oh, Lana, what have you done?" She reached across the table and grabbed her sister's hand in hers.

Lana raised her chin defensively. "I've done exactly what I wanted to do. More than anything in this world, I want a baby, and you know, Maya, there's never been a man in my life…at least nobody special. This seemed like the perfect way for both Chance and myself to get what we want. Once I get pregnant, Chance is going to sell this place and go back to the Midwest, and I'll return to my apartment in town and raise my child."

Maya released Lana's hand, a troubled frown on her pretty face. "I don't believe this. I've seen you with Chance, I've seen the way you look at him. Lana, when he leaves here, he's going to leave you pregnant and brokenhearted."

"Don't be ridiculous," Lana scoffed with a forced lightness.

"But you loved him when you were young."

"For heaven's sake, Maya, that was nothing but puppy love," Lana replied. "I had my eyes wide-open when I went into this agreement. Chance isn't making any false promises to me and I expect absolutely nothing from him except a pregnancy."

Lana picked up her fork once again and ate the piece of tomato, aware of her sister's gaze lingering on her. There was no way on earth Lana would continue her confession by admitting that she was again, still, hopelessly in love with Chance.

Her pride would not allow her to tell her sister that it was already too late for her to guard her heart against Chance. He'd already taken possession of it, invaded every one of her senses and indelibly marked her soul.

Still aware of Maya's gaze on her, Lana looked at her sister once again. "Please, no lectures. I already got one from Mama when I explained to her what I was going to do—although I just told her that I was marrying Chance so he could get his ranch. I didn't mention the baby part to her."

Maya finally smiled. "You're going to make a wonderful mother," she said.

Lana smiled gratefully. The rest of their lunch conversation was light and easy, and by one-thirty, Maya was gone, leaving Lana alone in the house.

In the month she'd been here, the place had begun to feel like home. Her apartment had always felt like a holding area, a temporary place to keep her things until she began her real life.

However, she knew the dangers of thinking of this house as a home. Eventually, probably in the next month or two, she'd be back in her apartment, and these days and weeks with Chance would only be a memory to make her happy—and make her sad.

As she cleaned up the lunch dishes, rain pelted the windows and the kitchen grew grayer and more gloomy. She put on a pot roast, then got a book from her room and curled up on the sofa.

The rain pitter-pattering against the windowpanes made her feel snug and safe and warm. She'd only been reading for about an hour when Chance came through the front door.

"Whew!" he exclaimed, shaking off the rain that clung to him. "It's a regular toad-strangler out there."

Lana sat up and placed her book on the coffee table. "But it sounds nice against the roof and the windows."

Chance shed his wet windbreaker and hung it on the hall tree, then paced the area in front of the sofa. "The weather forecasters all say it's supposed to move out in a couple of hours. There's nothing I can do for the time being except wait it out."

"It's a nice afternoon to curl up with a good book," she said. "Rainy days are wonderful reading days."

"I don't want to read," he replied. His hair was wet against his scalp and emphasized the strength of his handsome features. His T-shirt was also damp, pulling across the broadness of his shoulders, and

Lana's fingers tingled as she remembered how those shoulders felt when bared to her touch.

"Maybe you could find a good show on television," Lana said, her mouth suddenly dry as she saw the familiar look in his eyes.

"I'm not much of a TV buff," he said, then sat on the sofa next to her. "You know what I think?" He reached out to twirl a strand of her hair between two fingers.

"What?" she asked. His sinfully long dark eyelashes were spiky with dampness and his eyes beckoned her to fall into their green mist.

"I think it's a nice day to curl up with a good husband."

She felt his touch as if it were an electrical impulse shooting from the ends of her hair to her head, then down to the pit of her stomach.

"I can always read later," she murmured, her voice holding the breathless quality it always had when he touched her, when he gazed at her with want in his eyes.

"Good, because I don't want to wait until later to do this." He leaned forward and captured her mouth with his.

"How about one last cup of coffee before I head home?" Samuel Wallons, one of Red River's eldest citizens gestured to the cup before him.

"You got it," Emily replied with a friendly smile. She liked Samuel, who came in most afternoons and passed the time by telling tales of years gone by.

She poured him a fresh cup of coffee, then looked

at her wristwatch. Ten more minutes and she could go home. Although it was just a little after three in the afternoon, she was ready to call it a day.

Too little sleep, too many dreams the night before and an unusually busy lunch rush had left her exhausted. Her feet were killing her, her back ached, and all she wanted now was to go back to her quiet little cottage and take a long, refreshing nap.

"Emma?" The name rode above the din of the café and it took a moment for Emily to remember that was the name she'd been using.

Emma Logan. A fake name for a woman in hiding.

She looked around to see who was calling her. "Telephone." One of the busboys gestured to the kitchen where the phone was located.

Telephone? She frowned. Who would be calling her here? She hurried to the kitchen and grabbed the receiver.

"Hello?" she said and pressed the phone closer against her ear in an effort to hear over the kitchen din.

"Hello?" she repeated.

Silence.

Not the silence of a dead phone, but rather the screaming silence of somebody listening, but not speaking. "Is somebody there?" she asked, although she knew somebody was…she could sense their presence, hear them breathing. "Please…who is this?" She hesitated a moment. "Toby? Is that you?"

There was an audible click, and Emily knew she was alone on the line. Had Toby finally convinced

Wyatt to tell him where she was? Where she was working?

"Oh, Toby," she breathed softly, knowing she was going to have to go back to Keyhole, she was going to have to go back to let Toby know he needed to let her go.

Seven

Chance wondered when the time would come when he'd finally have had enough of her, when her hot kisses and silky skin no longer sent shooting flames of desire through him.

He didn't wonder *if* the time would come, only *when*. For there was one thing Chance was certain of: nothing good ever lasted. But, at the moment, none of these thoughts were important. His head was filled with Lana.

She returned his kiss with the same kind of fevered response that swept through him. Her mouth was sweet as honey, and he drank deeply of her, as if she alone offered him the nectar of life.

He allowed the kiss to linger for long minutes, then swept her up into his arms and carried her from the living room and into their bedroom.

With one hand he yanked down the bedspread, then placed her on the bed, as always thrilling at the sight of her long dark hair, and her chestnut skin against the white of the sheets.

Her dark eyes glittered and her lips were slightly parted, as if anticipating his next kiss. Blood rushed to his head, thick and hot, making any thought impossible.

It took him less than ten seconds to get out of his clothes and join her on the bed, where he once again claimed her mouth with his as his fingers moved to the buttons that ran down the front of her dress.

With each inch of her flesh that was revealed by the unfastening of the buttons, Chance's desire for her inched higher and higher. As she raised her hips to help him remove the dress and her lacy panties, he thought he might shatter with the wanting of her.

She was fire against him, and with the gentle patter of the rain on the roof as background music, Chance made love to her slowly.

He caressed her as if he had all the minutes of the day, all the hours of a year, until she was breathless and gasping and clutching him in sweet surrender.

Always before, when they were finished, they rolled apart, as if needing physical distance to maintain emotional distance. This time Chance didn't want to let her go.

Instead of allowing her to move away from him, he pulled her against him and held her, her breath warming the side of his neck as one of his hands stroked the smooth skin of her lower back.

She fit neatly against him, one leg thrown over his,

her soft breasts pressed against his ribs. Her long, silky hair was a spill across his chest and he thought he'd never felt anything quite so sensual before.

He was grateful that she didn't talk. He didn't want to speak, he merely wanted to bask in her warmth and listen to the rain softly beating on the windows.

She cuddled closer against him, her heart marking time with his and in the steady, reassuring beat, Chance felt a contentment he'd never known before.

It wasn't just about the fact that they had incredibly good sex together. Chance had enjoyed good sex before with other women. But, with those other women, the moment the sex was finished, the act was complete.

He'd hold the woman he'd just made love to if he felt she needed it, but for him that afterglow, the lingering in an embrace, had never been necessary.

Now it felt necessary. As essential as breathing, as vital as eating or drinking. This emotion he felt, this strange serenity was something he'd never experienced before and something he'd never dreamed possible.

He didn't try to analyze it, he merely closed his eyes and reveled in it. Her fingers stroked the hair on his chest, the rhythmic light touching drawing him deeper and deeper into relaxation.

The dream came almost immediately. He knew it was a dream because his father sat on the front porch, and Chance knew someplace in the back of his mind, outside of the dream, that his father was dead and buried in the cemetery that could just barely be seen from the porch.

"What are you doing, boy? Playing house?" Tom "Sarge" Reilly laughed, his brilliant green eyes glittering with the hard light that always made Chance's stomach feel slightly sick. "Are you pretending you're man enough to be a rancher, a husband?"

"I don't want to be a rancher," Chance replied evenly. "I don't want anything to do with this place. Besides, I don't have to listen to you. You are dead, Dad. Dead and buried."

Sarge laughed again. "I might be dead on earth, but I'm still alive inside you. I'm in your blood, boy. In your thoughts and in your soul. And I'm not a bit surprised that you don't want to be a rancher."

Sarge leaned back in the chair and swiped a hand through his dark crew cut. "Ranching takes lots of work. Backbreaking work. You're soft, boy, too soft. I always told your ma when she was alive that she was making a damn whimpering sissy out of you."

"I'm no sissy," Chance exclaimed.

"It takes a special kind of man to be a rancher. You'd never make it."

"Hard work doesn't scare me," Chance protested.

Sarge laughed, the sarcastic, biting sound symbolic of Chance's childhood. "Hard work doesn't scare you because you run from it. Always have, always will. Anything worth having is worth working for, but you'll never have anything because you're lazy and useless and good for nothing."

The words cut deeper than any slap in the face, any punch in the gut. "That's not true." Chance's heart pained with the weight of those familiar words.

Sarge laughed again. "Sure it is. You even married

a woman who doesn't want you. She just wants your sperm. As soon as she's done with you, she'll throw you away. Because you aren't a keeper, boy. You're worthless.''

"I am not. I am not." Chance jumped out of his chair and moved toward his father, whose laughter was so loud it hurt his ears. "I am not!" he yelled, trying to be heard over that damnable laughter.

"Chance...Chance..."

He came awake with a start, gratefully aware that Lana had shaken him out of his painful dreamscape and back to reality.

He drew in a deep breath and released it slowly, orienting himself to the here and now. He drew another breath in an attempt to shove aside the residual pain the dream had wrought. "I'm all right," he said to Lana, who eyed him worriedly in the semidarkness of the room.

She reached up and gently shoved a strand of his hair from his forehead. "Are you sure? You were yelling. It must have been some nightmare."

The tenderness of her touch winged right through him, warming him after the coldness of the dream. "Yeah...a nightmare." The torment of the dream still raced through him and he wondered if he'd ever be able to exorcise his father from his head.

Her dark eyes shone with empathy as her hand moved from his forehead to his shoulder, lingering with a welcomed warmth. "Do you want to talk about it?"

Did he want to talk about it? He thought not. Somehow he felt that to talk about it out loud might give it more power. "No. It was just a dumb dream."

He sat up and raked a hand through his hair, trying to forget the familiar hurtful words his father had used in the dream and wondering why those sentiments, spoken so often, had never lost their power over him.

The rain had apparently moved off and pale early evening light whispered through the curtains. "What time is it?" he asked.

Lana sat up next to him, seemingly unselfconscious despite the bareness of her breasts. She glanced at the clock on her nightstand. "Just after six. You must be starving."

"I am hungry," he agreed.

"Give me about fifteen minutes and I'll have supper on the table." She left the bed and padded naked across the room to where he'd thrown her dress and underclothes while in the throes of passion.

At some point in the last month, she had become comfortable with him and her own nudity. They no longer dressed in separate rooms and Chance recognized they had reached a deeper level of intimacy and trust.

He watched her, enjoying the sight of her nakedness. He liked the upward thrust of her small breasts, the tapered waist and shapely buttocks. Her legs were long and muscled just enough to add attractive shapeliness.

After she dressed and left the bedroom, Chance lay back once again, this time his head filling with a picture of a pregnant, naked Lana.

Her breasts would get larger and her nipples would

darken. The slender waistline would disappear as the months of her pregnancy advanced. He knew with certainty she would be beautiful carrying a baby. His baby. And he wouldn't be around to see it.

Again the words his father had laughed in the dream came back to haunt him. Worthless. Not a keeper. Even if she had made any indication that she wanted this marriage to last, that she wanted him to be a part of her life, she was better off without him.

He didn't want to risk finding out that his father was right, that he was worthless, that he couldn't make a woman happy forever, that he would never have the skills to parent.

And in any case, Lana hadn't made any indication of wanting him to stick around. She'd had a childhood crush on him, but that didn't translate into the mature kind of love that bound two people for life.

Out of sorts, and irritated with his thoughts, Chance left the bedroom for a shower. The nightmare had unsettled him, as had his own thoughts.

Minutes later, he walked into the kitchen to see Lana finishing up the last touches to the table. "Perfect timing," she said, a smile lighting her features.

"As usual, everything looks great," he said as he took his seat. "You always make all the food look so attractive." It was true. A sprig of parsley decorated the top of the mashed potatoes, and pineapple spears rested on a bed of lettuce, adding a touch of color to the table.

Lana sat across from him. "My mother always says pretty food tastes better."

"I'm not sure about that," he replied. The truth

was, it was the little extra efforts she made, not only with each meal, but around the house as well, that somehow filled up a hole in Chance.

After they'd eaten, he helped her with the dinner dishes, then they took a cup of coffee and sat on the two chairs on the front porch.

"Hmm, I love the smell of the air after a rain," she said.

Chance drew a deep breath, filling his lungs with the odor of damp earth, late-blooming flowers and the faint scent of Lana's perfume. "Yeah, it does smell nice, doesn't it?" He sipped his coffee, and gazed at her.

She looked lovely with her dark hair slightly tousled from their nap and her gaze off in the distance, as if she were contemplating the years to come. She looked as if she belonged sitting on this porch.

She turned and looked at him, as if she'd felt his gaze lingering on her. For the first time since she'd approached him with her crazy idea of the two of them getting married, he wondered what her plans were for after he left.

"Do you intend to work after you get pregnant?" he asked.

"Eventually, but probably not for the first year or so after the birth."

"Financially, how are you going to do it? I mean, I know you aren't independently wealthy, Lana."

She laughed. "Not even close. I live fairly frugally, and I have enough money set aside to allow me to take some time off and not worry about working." Her eyes gleamed with a softness. "It's important to me to spend at least the first year being a full-time mommy.''

He thought of how she'd tried to comfort him after his nightmare, the loving expression that had lit her face when she'd stroked the wood of the canopied crib in the store. ''You're going to make a wonderful mother,'' he said.

Her eyes lit and her cheeks pinkened. As always he found her easy blush charming. ''Thank you,'' she said simply. ''I certainly hope so. If I can be half the mother to my child that my mother was to me, I'll be satisfied.'' She took a sip of her coffee, then eyed him curiously. ''Tell me about your mother. You've never really talked about her before.''

Chance's first impulse was to refuse. What few memories he had of his mother he'd never shared with anyone. Not even years ago, when he and Lana had been confidantes, had Chance discussed his mother.

But now his mind opened to those memories. Sweet, warm memories. He leaned back in his chair and smiled. ''I remember she loved to sing. I'd wake up in the morning to the sound of her singing and the scent of bacon frying. And for just that moment, I'd feel safe and secure.''

''Did she have a nice voice?''

A bubble of laughter escaped him. ''Not really. She was slightly tone-deaf, but that didn't stop her. She didn't care who heard her. When she felt like singing, she sang.'' His laughter faded and he grew serious.

''What I remember most about her is that she was my champion, my defender against my father.''

"What do you mean?" Lana leaned forward slightly, her attention solely focused on him.

That was one of the things he'd liked about her even when she was a young girl. She had the ability to focus in on a person and make them feel as if what they were saying was important to her.

"I remember one time in particular. I was about seven, and my father decided it was time he take me hunting. I didn't want to go, I didn't have the stomach for shooting anything. Dad threw a fit, screaming and yelling at me, and my mother told him to leave me alone. And to my surprise, Dad did leave me alone."

The memory of his mother's arms around him after his father had stomped off, angrily branding him a "sissy," now sent a rivulet of warmth and love through him.

Lana leaned over and took his hand in hers. Her delicate fingers entwined with his and her eyes were soft and dewy, filled with compassion. "I'm sorry, Chance. I'm sorry she had to leave you. I know you must have missed her terribly."

He nodded, emotion too thick in his throat to allow him to speak. Yes, he'd missed his mother. He'd missed her off-key singing and her soft touches, he'd missed her protection and her laughter. And there were still days when the pain of her loss filled him.

But at the moment the pain felt real and immediate as he realized he would miss all of this when he left here. He'd miss sitting on the porch and watching the sunset. He'd miss the smell of the ranch and the burn of muscles from work.

He wouldn't be around to hear the sound of cattle

lowing from the pasture and the snort of horses in the corral. He'd miss walking the ranch at twilight and reflecting on a day well spent.

And, for the first time, he admitted to himself another truth. He would miss Lana.

Lana remained in bed, waiting for a wave of nausea to pass. For the past three mornings she'd awakened with a rolling tummy and the knowledge that if she moved too quickly, she'd be sick.

The first morning she'd assumed she'd caught a touch of a flu bug that had been making the rounds in the community. Yesterday morning she'd decided that perhaps the barbecue they'd eaten the night before had been too rich. This morning her heart pounded with the unsteady rhythm of uncertainty.

Was it possible? Now that she thought about it, she hadn't had a period since before their wedding. That knowledge, coupled with the early-morning queasiness made her wonder if perhaps she might be pregnant.

She touched her tummy, a curious mixture of excitement and just a tad of dread coursing through her. She was excited because it was possible she was finally going to achieve her dream of being a mother, but the dread came from knowing that if she was pregnant it would be the end of her marriage to Chance.

For six weeks she had been Chance's wife. September had gone and October had brought slightly cooler nights and a deepening love in her for the man who was her temporary husband.

When she told him she was pregnant, their bargain would be fulfilled and their lives together would be over. There would be no more reason for them to kiss, to touch, to make love.

Chance had almost finished the work on the outside of the ranch and had told her the previous day that before the week was over he'd be fixing the odds and ends in the house to get it ready for sale.

It was coming to an end, and even though she knew the right thing to do was to tell Chance immediately that she thought he'd fulfilled his end of the deal, she hugged the knowledge of her condition tightly inside and decided to wait a few days.

She knew why she wanted to wait. She wasn't ready to leave the marriage. She wasn't ready to leave him. She was praying for a miracle. She was praying he'd fall in love with her, realize he couldn't live without her. She was praying their marriage would become a real one, with a future of "until death do us part."

And she knew she was being a total fool in hoping something might change between them. Aware that the nausea had passed somewhat, she decided to get out of bed.

Moments later as she stood beneath a warm shower, she once again touched her stomach, wondering if already Chance's baby was inside her.

Chance's baby. When she'd first contemplated getting pregnant, she'd never considered a father. In all of her thoughts, it was always *her* baby.

But now she couldn't separate the man from the baby. It was and always would be Chance's baby,

GET 2

HOW TO GET YOUR
2 FREE BOOKS AND FREE GIFT!

1. Peel off the MIRA sticker on the front cover. Place it in the space provided at right. This automatically entitles you to receive two free books and an exciting surprise gift.

2. Send back this card and you'll get 2 "The Best of the Best™" novels. These books have a combined cover price of $11.98 or more in the U.S. and $13.98 or more in Canada, but they are yours to keep absolutely FREE!

3. There's no catch. You're under no obligation to buy anything. We charge nothing – ZERO – for your first shipment. And you don't have to make any minimum number of purchases – not even one!

4. We call this line "The Best of the Best" because each month you'll receive the best books by some of today's most popular authors. These authors show up time and time again on all the major bestseller lists and their books sell out as soon as they hit the stores. You'll like the convenience of getting them delivered to your home at our special discount prices . . . and you'll love your *Heart to Heart* subscriber newsletter featuring author news, horoscopes, recipes, book reviews and much more!

5. We hope that after receiving your free books you'll want to remain a subscriber. But the choice is yours – to continue or cancel, anytime at all! So why not take us up on our invitation, with no risk of any kind. You'll be glad you did!

6. And remember...we'll send you a surprise gift ABSOLUTELY FREE just for giving "The Best of the Best" a try.

SPECIAL FREE GIFT!

We'll send you a fabulous surprise gift, absolutely FREE, simply for accepting our no-risk offer!

Visit us online at
www.mirabooks.com

Chance's child. It was possible the baby would have his green eyes and square-shaped face. It was possible the baby would be a spitting image of Chance. And he wanted no part of it.

She finished her shower, dressed in a pair of jeans and a T-shirt, then left the bathroom and headed for the kitchen. She was surprised to see Chance there, the top half of his body inside the cabinet beneath the sink.

"Good morning," she said.

He jumped and banged his head on a pipe. "Ouch! Good morning."

Lana stifled a giggle and leaned down. "Sorry if I startled you."

He flashed the white of his teeth in a grin. "It's all right, you just gave me a concussion, but I'll be fine once the whirling stars go away."

"What are you doing?" she asked.

"I thought I'd fix the faucet, but when I got down here I found a leak, so I'm working on that first."

"Is there anything I can do to help?"

"Yeah, help me out of here so I can have a cup of coffee before I finish this."

Lana grabbed his hand and giggled as he once again banged his head before finally crawling out from beneath the sink. She helped pull him to his feet and laughed again as she reached up and finger-combed his messy hair. "You look like you've been working hard, Mr. Reilly."

He grinned at her. "And you look like a lazy woman who slept late, Mrs. Reilly," he returned.

"Guilty as charged," she replied, her heart thrilling

at the light, teasing glint in his eyes. So often his eyes
were stormy seas of intense emotions and she knew
he was thinking of his father. But at the moment all
was calm and his eyes were the sweet green of spring.

"You want coffee?" he asked as he stepped away
from her and went to the counter that held the cof-
feemaker.

"I don't think so." The very thought of drinking
a cup made her stomach roll in protest. "But I'll sit
with you while you drink yours." She sat at the table
and watched him get his cup.

She wondered if there would ever come a time
when she didn't thrill to the sight of him. As always,
his tight, worn jeans perfectly formed to the length of
his legs and slender hips. His T-shirt pulled taut
against the width of his shoulders and hugged his flat
abdomen tightly.

On the trips they'd taken into town in the past six
weeks, she hadn't missed the admiring glances of the
women around him. Waitresses simpered, store clerks
giggled and even older women's gazes lingered on
him.

Not for the first time, she wondered if he'd left a
special someone back in the Midwest. Was there a
woman in one of those small towns he traveled
through eagerly waiting his return? When he made
love to Lana so sweetly, so tenderly, was he thinking
of another woman? A woman he'd left behind in order to claim this ranch?

As he joined her at the table, she drew a deep
breath and decided the only way to find out was to

ask. "Chance? Was there somebody special you were seeing in one of those little towns in Kansas?"

"Somebody special?" He shook his head. "No, nobody. Why do you ask?"

She wanted to tell him she'd asked because she loved him, loved him with all her heart and soul. She desperately wanted to tell him that she wanted their marriage to be real, to last forever, and if he wanted to sell this place and go back to the midwest, she'd go with him. She'd go wherever he wanted, if he would just love her.

She needed to know if the reason he wasn't sticking around here was because he was already in love with somebody and he was just marking time here until he could return to that special someone. But she didn't say any of this. "Just curious," she finally replied, although she had no idea what she hoped to gain with the information.

She only knew now her competition for a lifetime with Chance wasn't another woman. Her obstacle to spending her future with him appeared to be nothing more than Chance himself. And she didn't know what to do about that—except to continue to love him for the time they had together.

Eight

Emily unlocked the door to the unfamiliar small cabin and flicked on the lights inside. The bright illumination was a welcome relief after the short walk through the wooded area from her car in the parking lot of the motel.

The Hollow Tree Motel was located on the outskirts of Keyhole and consisted of small cabins spread among thick trees. The advertisement on the highway had indicated clean, inexpensive and private.

She'd called Toby from a pay phone just outside town and had told him to meet her here in the morning. She knew she had to talk to him, to tell him that although she would always treasure his friendship and support, there would never be anything romantic between them. It was the least she could do for a man who had shown her kindness in her darkest hours.

She set her overnight bag on the floor and took a brief moment to familiarize herself with the cabin. It was a simple setup. A combination living room with kitchenette, a bathroom and a small, but adequate bedroom. Although certainly nothing luxurious, it was fine for one night, and that's only as long as she intended to be here.

Kicking off her shoes, she flopped down on the sofa and drew a deep breath. She was exhausted. She'd pulled a double shift at the diner, then had hopped into the car to make the trip from Red River to this motel in Keyhole.

Thinking of the conversation she had to have with Toby the next morning only made her more exhausted...and sad. It would be one of the most difficult things she'd ever done in her life, and for the hundredth time, she wished her heart had been able to love Toby. And she did love him, but not in the way he needed to be loved.

Her thoughts turned to her mother, Meredith. As difficult as Emily's life had been from the time Patsy had orchestrated the car crash and pretended to be Meredith, Emily couldn't imagine what Meredith's life must have been like.

It must be horrid to have no memories of any family, of the past shared with loved ones. Meredith had lost everything. Her family. Her friends. Her memories. She had been utterly alone in the world after the car accident.

Still, Meredith had been strong enough to make a life for herself. Emily knew she had been working in an office job at the University of Mississippi and lived in a house where she had a little garden.

Emily might have temporarily been displaced from her home. She might have momentarily lost her family, but at least she had her memories.

A smile curved her lips upward as she remembered how much her mother had loved working in the large garden at the ranch. Meredith and Marco Ramirez, the Colton gardener, had often spent long hours discussing various flowers and plants.

A vision of Meredith filled Emily's head. It was a vision of her wearing an old pair of jeans and one of her husband's shirts, gardening spade in hand as she planted in the garden that surrounded a huge fountain in the center of the courtyard.

And soon she'll be back at the ranch and gardening there, Emily told herself, refusing to believe in any possibility other than a happy ending.

Her heart crashed into her chest as a knock fell on her door. She glanced at her watch. Almost eleven. Surely the manager of the place wouldn't be bothering her at this time of night. There was only one other person it could be.

Toby.

She peered out the window next to the door. Even in the darkness of the night, she recognized his silhouette, tall and lean. She opened the door.

"Emma." He swept off his hat as he stepped through the door and set it on the nearby coffee table. A tentative smile lit his boyishly handsome face. "I...I couldn't wait until tomorrow to see you. I have been worried about you. I'll come back in the morn-

ing if you want...I just...I just needed to see you."
His blue eyes gazed at her with warmth and confusion. "You left here without a word. I just had to see that you were okay."

"I'm fine, Toby." She knew the best thing to do would be to talk to him right now, to tell him that she cared about him, but would never be the woman in his life. But, she didn't feel prepared at the moment. She'd intended to pick and choose her words carefully throughout this night before speaking them to him in the morning. "Toby, I'm really too tired to talk tonight, but I'll see you in the morning at ten like we planned!"

"Sure," he agreed instantly. "That will be fine. How about if I bring breakfast with me?"

Emily hesitated then nodded. "That would be nice," she said. "Then I'll see you in the morning."

"Sleep well, Emma," he said with a last, lingering sweet smile, then he turned and left.

Emily closed and locked the door behind him, her heart heavy as she anticipated the morning to come. Once again she sank down on the sofa, her thoughts drifting back to the time she'd spent in Keyhole.

Her relationship with Toby was based on a series of lies. Initially, he'd believed she was part of a car theft ring operating in a nearby town. But, finally he'd come to believe the story she'd told him, that her name was Emma Logan and she'd lost her fiancé in a tragic car accident and had come to Keyhole, Wyoming to heal her broken heart.

It hadn't taken her long to realize he was a sweet, gentle man. He'd often talked about his older brother,

Josh, who worked the rodeo circuit and Emily had enjoyed him telling stories of the two when they had been young.

The bed looked wonderfully inviting as she entered the bedroom and she was just about to undress for the night when a soft knock fell on her front door.

Toby. He'd remembered his hat.

She hurried to the door and started to open it, then cried out as it was flung open with a force that threw her backward and nearly off her feet.

Horror swept through her, chilling her to the bone, etching terror into her heart as she stared at the man who stood before her.

Long, sandy-colored hair was pulled back in a ponytail, revealing a balding place on the top of his head. He was rather thin, with a slightly protruding pot belly. His Fu-Manchu-style mustache and goatee drew attention to his thin mouth...a mouth now smiling and exposing a large space between his two front teeth. In his hand, he held a gun.

Although she had no idea what his name was, she knew who he was, had seen him twice before when she'd barely escaped with her life. He was the man her aunt Patsy had hired to kill her.

"Well, if it isn't little Emily Blair...or would you rather I call you Emma Logan?" His dark eyes gleamed as he shoved the door shut behind him, then advanced closer to where she stood.

He walked with a limp, and someplace in the back of her mind, Emily thought that if she could just get away from him, she could outrun him. However, at the moment she didn't attempt to run as she knew it was impossible for her to outrun a speeding bullet.

"Who are you? What do you want?" Somewhere in the back of her mind she knew she was stalling...hoping...praying for a miracle.

"The name is Silas Pike, but my friends call me Snake Eyes." He grinned again, as if he liked the sound of his nickname.

Snake Eyes. Yes, she could understand why he was called that. His eyes, so dark they were almost black, were small and beady and held the same kind of malevolent blankness she'd seen in snakes.

Her gaze darted away from his, seeking, searching for something nearby that could be used as a weapon. But what made an adequate weapon against a gun?

"What do you want?" she asked, her voice slightly trembling. "If it's money, I have a little bit. I'll get it for you and you can leave. I won't tell anyone you were here or report you to the police."

He laughed, the sound unpleasant and sending a new chill shimmering up her spine. "I'll take your money after I do what I've been hired to do." He seemed in no hurry to accomplish what he'd come for. He walked around the room, his gaze darting here and there.

"Patsy hired you, didn't she? Patsy Portman?"

"I don't know any Patsy. I was hired by a woman named Meredith. Course, she didn't tell me her name, but I did some checking and found out who she was."

Despair swept through Emily. Even though she'd suspected the truth, had feared it in her heart, the cer-

tain knowledge that Patsy had, indeed, hired this...
this Snake Eyes to kill her was devastating.

"I've been looking for you for a long time. If you'd
been ugly, I might not have found you. But folks
remember a pretty young woman with pretty long
hair." He smiled slyly. "And I've seen you cozying
up to that local yokel deputy sheriff. Too bad it didn't
do you any good."

Silas stepped closer to her, close enough that she
could smell him—the smell of stale body odor and
sour breath, the smell of evil and imminent death.

"You've been a bad girl." His voice was soft and
his smile remained on his face. "You've wasted a lot
of my time. You were supposed to be dead months
ago."

"Please, Mr. Pike. Whatever she's paid you, I'll
double it if you just turn around and walk away from
here."

She knew it was no good to scream. The other cabins were empty and nobody would hear her. Nobody
would even hear the gun when he shot it and sent a
bullet through her. Oh, why hadn't she taken a room
in town?

"That's real nice," he said. "The way you called
me Mr. Pike, all respectful-like. But I'm afraid it's
less a matter of money and more a matter of honor.
I was hired to do a job, and I don't want word to get
around that I don't do what I promise to do."

A bubble of hysterical laughter rose to her throat.
A hired killer who was afraid of gossip. The laughter
quickly transformed to tears.

She would die here alone in this cottage, away from

the family she loved, never to see her mother finally regain her place in that family.

"Those tears won't change my mind," he said, a touch of derisiveness in his voice. "Let's just get this done, so I can get out of this one-horse town," he finally said wearily.

"Turn around," he instructed.

Emily drew a deep shuddering breath. "No."

He looked at her in surprise.

"I won't turn around. I won't make it easy on you by letting you shoot me in the back." She raised her chin, once again praying for a miracle. "You're going to have to look me in the eyes when you pull that trigger and kill me."

He frowned, obviously not pleased with her words. Then he shrugged. "It don't make no matter to me," he said. He raised the gun and a rush of adrenaline soared through Emily.

Before he could pull the trigger, she leapt over and behind the sofa. She hit the floor, painfully jarring her elbow and knocking the breath from her.

She'd rather be killed while doing something constructive than shot standing still like a deer frozen in a car's headlights.

"Dammit, why are you making this so hard? Say your prayers, Emily Colton." He laughed, obviously amused by his tough-guy line. The laughter chilled Emily to her bones. "Here I come, and nothing is gonna stop me now." The words were followed by a loud crash.

"Emma!"

Toby's voice was nearly swallowed by the sharp report of gunshots. Two shots in rapid succession.

Then silence.

Emily held her breath, her entire body shaking as she waited to hear a sound, any sound that would let her know what had just occurred. Seconds passed and she stuffed her fist against her mouth to still the cries of terror that begged to be released.

Finally, she heard something—a soft, almost inaudible moan.

She peeked her head up over the back of the sofa and cried out in horror as she saw Toby sprawled on the floor near the front door, a crimson stain spreading over the front of his khaki shirt. Silas "Snake Eyes" Pike was nowhere to be seen.

"Toby!" She pulled herself up off the floor and raced around the edge of the sofa. She fell to the floor beside him, her heart thundering in her chest.

Oh God. Oh God. Oh God. The words reverberated in her brain. She could tell his wound was bad. Really bad. Blood was seeping not only from his chest, but puddling on the floor beneath him. "Oh God, Toby."

He smiled at her, a brief, quicksilver smile. "I forgot my hat."

She nodded, tears racing down her cheeks. His blue eyes gazed at her worriedly and he reached for her hand. "Did...did he hurt you?" he asked, his voice whispery soft.

"No...no. He didn't hurt me." She tried to pull away from him. "I've got to get you help."

"Too...late," he said, the shine in his eyes fading and his voice even more weak. "You...have to get out of here. He…ran out, but I don't know if I shot him.''

"I'm not leaving you,'' she exclaimed and once again tried to pull her hand from his.

He released her hand and touched her cheek softly. "Don't fret…just get out of here. Everything is going to be all right, Emma.'' His hand dropped to his side, and his eyes continued to gaze at her, only this time his gaze was blank.

"Toby?'' She grabbed his hand, but there was no reciprocating movement in his. "Toby!'' With trembling fingers she touched the side of his neck, trying desperately to feel a pulse.

Nothing. And his eyes continued to stare. She realized he was gone. Dead.

Deep, wrenching sobs overtook her as she held his hand, drew it to her lips and kissed it. Oh God, not Toby. Please, bring him back. Don't take him. Sweet, dear Toby, who had always looked out for her, who had suspected she might be in trouble.

Dead.

Dead because of her.

She wasn't sure how long she sat beside him, gripping his hand and sobbing, but through the grief that ripped through her, fear once again flurried inside her and she knew she had to do as Toby had told her to. She had to get out of here.

She pulled herself up, knowing there was nothing more she could do for Toby, and grabbed her purse and duffelbag.

Tears half blinded her as she glanced down at the body. "I'm sorry, Toby,'' she whispered. "I'm so sorry.'' The grief that filled her was nearly debilitating, but she shoved it away. "You're a hero, Toby. You'll always be my hero.''

A moment later she slipped out of the cottage and into the dark of the night. She paused there, swallowing again and again in an effort to still her sobs. She had to put her grief aside and focus on her present situation.

She had no idea if Toby had managed to shoot Silas Pike. She couldn't know if the gunman was now lying in a pool of blood or if he'd managed to escape Toby's shot unscathed.

She had no idea if Silas had come alone or had brought an accomplice with him. It was possible Silas or one of his cohorts was hiding behind one of the trees, squatted down in the underbrush, waiting for her, waiting to finish his job.

He wouldn't know that Toby was dead, that Toby could no longer protect her. But, eventually, if he were capable, he would realize something was amiss and he would return to the cottage to complete what he'd begun.

She crept from tree to tree, holding her breath and trying not to step on branches or twigs that might snap and give away her location. Her anguish over Toby was shoved deep inside, her instinct for survival first and foremost at the moment.

Walking as swiftly and as silently as she could, she kept her ears peeled for any sound, no matter how small, that might indicate Silas "Snake Eyes" Pike was following her.

She headed for the highway. Even though she knew

hitchhiking was dangerous, it didn't seem as dangerous as the man who might be stalking her. And at the moment a car or truck carrying her far away from here sounded wonderful.

Still, it was slow going as she found herself freezing, heart pounding, each time she heard a crackling of underbrush or the wind rustling leaves.

She wasn't sure how much time passed or how long she had walked before she finally came to the highway. Hiding behind a tree some distance away, she eyed the deserted road and prayed for headlights to pierce the darkness of the night.

It was as she was crouched in the underbrush by the highway that a new thought sent terror through her. What if Silas Pike had a car? What if he was parked down the highway at this very moment, watching, waiting for her to emerge from the brush?

Nine

"I thought I'd surprise you and make breakfast," Chance said when Lana entered the kitchen. He walked toward her, a pleased smile on his handsome face as he held a plate of eggs, sausage and toast under her nose.

Lana took one look, the odors of grease and food wafting to her nose, and backed away from him and the plate. She turned and raced to the bathroom, slammed the door behind her, then was violently ill.

She'd managed to hide the morning sickness from Chance for the past week because when she got out of bed in the mornings, he was already outside.

By the time he came into the house around noon for lunch, the brief bout of sickness had passed and she was fine for the remainder of the day.

Now, feeling as if the worst was behind her, she rinsed her mouth and brushed her teeth, disappointment sweeping through her as she realized the cat was probably now out of the bag. He would know that he'd successfully fulfilled his end of their bargain.

She stared at her reflection in the mirror, but saw no discernible sign of pregnancy. She'd heard of the glow of pregnancy, but after spilling her guts, her skin retained a paleness that didn't even begin to resemble a glow.

She opened the bathroom door, unsurprised to see Chance standing in the hallway. "I've had some interesting reactions to my cooking, but I think that was probably the most dramatic," he said with a touch of wry humor.

"I'm sorry," she replied, a touch of nausea still rolling in the pit of her stomach. She drew in a deep breath in an attempt to calm herself and still her bucking tummy.

"Do you think maybe you have a touch of the flu?" He gazed at her intently, his facial expression utterly unreadable.

She considered saying yes, telling a little white lie that would extend their time together, but she knew she couldn't. "No, I don't think it's the flu."

"What do you think it might be?"

He knew. She could see in his eyes that he knew what it was, but he was waiting for her to speak it, to say the words out loud.

"I think maybe it's morning sickness."

Finally speaking the words out loud sent a thrill through her, an excited thrill tempered by the devastating knowledge that there would now be no reason for Chance to ever make love to her again.

"Morning sickness," he echoed. "Maybe we should get one of those home pregnancy tests to make sure. We should probably do that before we make a doctor's appointment for you."

"Okay," she agreed, surprised that he'd used "we" instead of "you," making it obvious he intended to be a part of this at least until they got the final results and knew for certain that she was pregnant.

Together they went back into the kitchen, where Chance had apparently removed any sign of food while she'd been in the bathroom. "How about just a piece of toast or maybe a couple of crackers?" he asked.

"No, thanks, I'm fine for a little while." She sank down at the table, still feeling a little shaky.

"What about a cup of coffee? A glass of juice or something?" His brow wrinkled worriedly.

She waved her hands, then smiled at him reassuringly. "I'm fine, Chance. My stomach should settle down by noon, then I'll eat some lunch."

He sat down at the table across from her, his brow still crinkled worriedly. "Are you feeling all right other than the nausea? I mean, are you in any pain or anything like that?"

"No. Really, I'm fine." His obvious concern touched her deep inside and sent a warm glow through her. He cared. At least he cared a little bit about her.

"Do you want to go ahead and take a ride into town? Get the test?"

"I don't want to interfere with your work schedule," she replied.

He shrugged. "I probably won't get much done until we find out what's going on with you. We might as well head on into town."

"Okay," she said without enthusiasm, knowing that a positive test result would be the final nail in the coffin of her marriage. "Just let me get my purse."

She left the kitchen and went back into their bedroom. She grabbed her purse, but hesitated in the doorway, gazing at the bed where Chance had introduced her to such physical pleasure. It wasn't just his lovemaking that she was going to miss.

She'd miss his quicksilver, sexy smile, the laughter that transformed his eyes to a beautiful spring green. She'd miss sitting on the porch with him in the evenings, sharing the end of the day with quiet conversation and reflective thoughts.

Grief ripped through her, unexpected in its intensity. She'd known for some time that it would be difficult for them to part, but she hadn't realized just how difficult it was going to be.

Would he want her to leave immediately? By this evening, with a positive test result known, would she be packing her things? Would she awaken in the morning not with Chance's arms around her, but rather alone in the bed in her lonely apartment?

She left the bedroom and shoved these thoughts away. She couldn't dwell on the future, not even the immediate future. She'd take this day minute by minute. She had a feeling it was the only way she would be able to get through it.

He was waiting for her by the front door, jingling his car keys in his hand. She wondered if he was eager to get the test, get the results, and then get her out of his life. Again a shaft of pain shot through her heart.

"Ready?" he asked.

"Ready," she replied and together they left the house that for Lana had become a home.

"You know the minute we buy a home pregnancy test in the drug store, everyone in town will know it," she said once they were in the car and on their way.

"Yeah, there aren't many secrets in Prosperino, are there? But I figure if you went to a doctor, everyone in town would also know."

She nodded her agreement. She well knew how gossip flew in Prosperino. For years the major topic of conversation in the café and between women at the stores had been the dramatic change in Meredith Colton's personality. Or, more recently, the attempted murder of Joe Colton and the arrest of his friend Emmett Fallon.

She wondered how much gossip had flown around about her and Chance following their quickie wedding? Everyone in Prosperino knew Chance as a sexy bad boy, a young man who'd often been in trouble with his father, and occasionally in trouble with the law. They knew him as a man who'd never committed himself to anyone or anything.

They saw only the shell he presented to the outside

world. But Lana knew the truth. She knew him as a sensitive man with a beautiful spirit, a man who had been scarred by the years of abuse inflicted on him by his father.

"Are you feeling better?" he asked, breaking into her thoughts.

"Yes, much." She grinned at him. "Don't worry, I promise I won't throw up in your car."

He returned her smile. "I wasn't worried about that." His smile faded. "I just don't like the idea of you feeling bad."

Oh, heaven help her. When he said nice things to her like that, her heart fluttered and her love for him expanded. She cast him a surreptitious glance, noting how wonderful he looked in the dark green, long-sleeved dress shirt. The color brought out the bright green of his eyes and pulled forth the golden strands in his brown hair.

Aware that her time with him was running out, she tried to memorize each and every feature—the square shape of his face, his strong, straight nose, the full lips that gave him a sensual, sexy aura.

She directed her gaze out the window, in her mind's eye seeing his naked body, the broad shoulders dusted lightly with a sprinkling of freckles, the muscled chest with its soft golden hair and the flat abdomen with a tiny mole right next to his belly button.

His legs were long and muscular and covered with springy, curly hairs that pleasantly tickled her legs when he wrapped them around her.

Her inner temperature seemed to climb higher as

she thought of him more intimately, remembering the nights of pleasure he'd given her, the mastery of his caresses, the control that allowed him to take her to the peak over and over again before sating himself.

And beyond the intensity of her physical reaction to him, she knew she'd miss those moments when he'd walk past her and lightly touch her hair or give her back a quick stroke. She'd miss the way he placed his hand in the small of her back when they crossed a street, how he always held out a hand to help her up out of a chair. He did these things unconsciously, but she was intensely conscious of every single touch from him.

She tried to imagine herself in the future, alone and raising Chance's son or daughter. Would the child look like him? Would her daughter have bright green eyes, or her son have Chance's square facial shape and strong nose? Would she be able to look at her baby and not remember, not mourn for the man she loved?

Again she worked to push these disturbing thoughts out of her head, unwilling to grieve before it was absolutely, positively necessary. At least she had a little bit of time with him before they knew the test results and they told each other goodbye.

Once they reached town, Chance was in no hurry to race to the drugstore and buy the test. He suddenly thought of a dozen errands he'd been putting off but now seemed necessary to complete immediately.

It was an additional pleasure to have Lana tagging along. In the hardware store she helped him pick out the new handles he wanted to put on the kitchen cabinets. He listened to her opinions, remembering what she'd said about needing to please a prospective buyer's wife as well as the husband.

He appreciated her input on what was the best kind of floor cleaner to scrub the linoleum in the kitchen and which furniture polish did the best job.

And in every conversation, in every minute that passed between them, the knowledge that she was probably pregnant never got far from his mind.

Hearing her in the bathroom that morning had been torturous for him. He'd heard about morning sickness, but he'd never really thought about what it meant. Why on earth would women want to get pregnant and suffer through that kind of thing?

What other negative things would happen to her and her body during pregnancy? He'd heard of crazy cravings, intense mood swings and uncontrollable weeping. Would she be able to handle all that alone? Had she really understood what she'd been getting into when she'd agreed to this whole crazy scheme?

After the hardware store, he asked her if she felt like getting a bite to eat and she readily agreed. They went to the café and took a booth in the back. Within minutes Angie came out from the kitchen to visit with them.

"Hey, you two," she greeted them with her usual friendly smile. "I've been meaning to drive by your place for the last week or so." She plunged her hand into the pocket of her huge apron and withdrew several index cards and handed them to Lana.

"What's this?" Lana asked.

Angie smiled sheepishly. "I hope I'm not being presumptuous and I'm sure you're a wonderful cook. But these are the recipes for dishes I remember Chance especially loved eating here."

She smiled warmly at Chance. "I haven't forgotten how much you enjoyed my hot chicken salad when you were young, and that strawberry pie that I used to make." She turned and looked at Lana. "I just thought it would be nice if you, as his wife, had those recipes."

Lana's eyes were huge and impossibly luminous. "Thank you, Angie," she said, then suddenly bolted from the table and raced toward the rest rooms.

Angie looked at Chance in surprise. "My goodness, is she all right? Did I say something wrong?"

"No, nothing like that," Chance hurriedly assured her. "Lana has been fighting off a little flu bug for the past couple of days." The little white lie rolled from his lips effortlessly. He wasn't about to admit to Angie that Lana might be pregnant before they knew for sure.

"There's some nasty stuff going around," Angie replied. "I heard Wilma Nitters had to be hospitalized for dehydration after a bout with the flu."

"Trust me, I'll see that doesn't happen to Lana," Chance said.

Angie smiled at him. "I'm so happy for you, Chance. It's good to see you looking so happy." She reached out and patted his shoulder with her plump hand. "Me and Harmon drove by your ranch the other night and the place looks great. Your mama would have been proud of you. She loved that ranch.''

Chance looked at Angie in surprise. ''My mother loved the ranch?''

''Indeed.'' With no little effort, Angie scooted into the place Lana had vacated, her plump body just fitting between the back of the booth and the table. ''Ah, Chance, your mama loved that place almost as much as she loved you. Most evenings she'd sit on the porch and listen to the cattle, the insects, the night songs of birds and she told me she always felt secure, and warm and safe because she knew she was listening to the sounds of home. She'd be so pleased that you're carrying on her love of the land and making that place a home.''

Chance was positively amazed by this information. ''Why did you never tell me this before?''

Angie shrugged. ''When you were younger, all you wanted to do was escape from here. When you got older and came back to town for your brief visits, you still had the look of a wanderer in your eyes.''

Angie gazed at him thoughtfully, her sharp eyes seeming to peer right into his soul. ''I see a new maturity in you. Lana is good for you. Your mother would have embraced her like the daughter she never had.''

Chance frowned thoughtfully, trying to make sense of this new information. ''I never really thought about Mom liking the ranch.''

''Your father bought it because of her,'' Angie replied. ''I think Tom would have been perfectly satisfied to stay in the army forever. But your mother wanted a home, a ranch, and so your father left the army and bought the place to please her.''

They both looked up as Lana appeared once again. Angie quickly scooted out of the booth. ''You doing okay, sweetie?'' she asked as she patted Lana's shoulder. ''Chance said you've been fighting off a little flu bug.''

''I'm fine,'' Lana smiled sheepishly and slid back in across from Chance. He eyed her critically, noting that her eyes looked slightly puffy and red, as if she'd been crying.

''I'd better get back to the kitchen,'' Angie said. ''If I'm not back there supervising, no telling what the customers might be served.''

''Thank you, Angie,'' Lana said. ''It was very thoughtful of you to write out the recipe cards for me.''

Angie beamed a happy smile, then headed back to the kitchen.

''Are you sure you're all right?'' Chance asked Lana. ''We don't have to eat if you're still feeling sick.''

''No, I'm not feeling sick anymore.'' She picked up a fork and stared at it, as if unable to meet his gaze. ''I just suddenly got weepy, that's all. I guess it's some kind of a hormonal thing.''

A hormonal thing. ''Does that mean maybe you aren't pregnant, but that your hormones are just all screwed up?'' he asked.

"I really don't know, Chance," she said softly. "I guess we'll have the answer when I take the test."

They fell silent as the waitress appeared at their table to take their orders. As they waited for their food, Chance tried to figure out exactly what he felt about the possibility of her pregnancy.

On the one hand, he should be pleased that he had managed to give her what she wanted, had fulfilled his end of their bargain. On the other hand, he knew if she was now pregnant, she probably wouldn't want him making love to her anymore.

And that thought shouldn't bother him, after all, he'd known right from the start why she had allowed him to make love to her night after night—because she wanted a baby. There had never been any pretense of love between them. It had been a business arrangement.

But that didn't explain the disappointment that swept through him as he thought of never again holding Lana in his arms, never again feeling her soft sighs and sweet gasps against his throat.

He found his gaze drawn to her again and again as they ate. For some reason, she appeared far lovelier now than the day she had married him.

He wasn't sure what the difference was, only knew that there was a luminous glow to her skin, a certain knowing in her eyes, that transformed her from a sweetly attractive woman to a sexy, gorgeous, exciting woman.

"Angie told me something interesting while you

were in the rest room,'' he said, trying to empty his mind of thoughts of her.

''Really? What's that?''

''She told me my mother loved the ranch, that my father quit the army and bought the place just to please my mother.'' Again a sense of wonderment filled Chance as Angie's words played in his head.

Lana studied him thoughtfully. ''And you don't remember that about your mother?''

Chance frowned. For so many years he'd consciously shoved away memories of his mother, first angry with her for dying and leaving him alone with his father, then later finding the memories simply too painful to bear.

Now he reached back into his treasure chest of memories in an attempt to retrieve all those cherished images from his childhood.

''I told you before she sang a lot. In my memories she was always smiling or laughing. I remember she had a huge garden on the side of the house and loved planting vegetables and flowers there.'' He smiled, his heart suddenly filled with a warmth. ''She was like a ray of sunshine. Even my dad wasn't too bad when she was there.''

''Maybe losing her is what made your father such an angry, bitter man,'' Lana observed. ''If what Angie said is true, your father gave up his dream of the army life for her, then she died.''

Chance frowned. ''That doesn't excuse what he did to me over the years.''

''You're right,'' she agreed quickly. ''There is no

excuse for what your father did to you, but perhaps that's an explanation."

"Maybe," Chance finally replied. Even trying to understand why his father had been so miserable, so cruel to him, didn't ease any of the pain those particular memories wrought.

They finished eating, then left the café and went directly to the drugstore. Chance was amazed by the variety of pregnancy tests that were available. He picked up first one box, then another, wanting to buy the best and most accurate.

"Do you know anything about these?" he asked Lana, who was also perusing the display with a bewildered expression.

She eyed him dryly, a twinkling in her dark eyes. "I'd never had sex before you, so I certainly am not an expert on pregnancy tests."

He wanted her then and there. An enormous desire swept through him, one greater than any he'd experienced before for her. For a brief moment it left him weak-kneed and half-breathless.

She stood there, holding a box in each hand, seemingly unaware of the volcanic want that nearly consumed him. For the first time that day, he noticed how her dress clung provocatively to her breasts, how the bright yellow color complemented her skin tones and made her eyes appear darker, mysteriously beckoning.

He grabbed one of the tests from her hand. "We'll get this one," he said and turned on his heels.

He was irritated with himself, wondering if his monumental desire for her at the moment was only because he knew there was a possibility he'd never possess her again.

He paid for the test, then stalked out of the drugstore, aware of Lana trailing behind him in silence.

As they walked back to his car, he cooled down, the grip of desire releasing him. He smiled at Lana, to assure her that all was okay.

She'd obviously sensed his tension, for the smile she returned to him was one of relief. Still, as they drove home, they were silent, as if the brown paper sack containing the pregnancy test on the seat between them had somehow stolen their small talk.

When they pulled down the lane that led to the ranch, for the first time in his life Chance really looked at the land and the buildings that, for the moment, were his.

The corral looked strong and sturdy and the barn looked as if it could withstand anything man or nature might throw its way. The pastures were lush, and here and there along the fences wild blackberry bushes grew.

"Do you know how to make jam?" he asked Lana suddenly.

"No, but I'm sure my mother knows how. Why?"

"I just remembered my mother and I used to walk down to those bushes and pick blackberries. She made great jam."

He smiled as the memory came to fruition in his mind. "She'd wear a big, old floppy straw hat and we'd pick blackberries until our hands were black with the juice. We'd pick a bucket full, then eat them right off the vine. She'd laugh and tell me that she bet the Coltons, with all their money and fine things, weren't as happy as we were just picking blackberries."

Lana leaned toward him and placed a hand on his forearm. "I'm glad you have good memories of her, Chance. You need to hang on to those."

He nodded and for the first time in his life wondered if perhaps he wasn't making a mistake in selling this place and returning to his rootless, vagabond life.

Ten

How had this happened? How had something that should have filled her with such joy suddenly become a catalyst for such heartbreak?

Lana stared intently at the small test window, her heart pounding as she waited to see if a plus sign appeared.

Plus sign, you're pregnant; minus sign you're not. At least Chance had picked an easy test to read. Plus, you lose the man you love; minus, you lose your heart's desire.

Even as this thought crossed her mind, she knew it wasn't as simple as that. She couldn't lose Chance, because she'd never really had him. For the past seven weeks, since the day she'd said "I do" to him, she might have pretended to herself that she had him, but that wasn't reality.

She'd allowed herself to fall in love with him, to entertain a small germ of hope that he might fall in love with her. She'd allowed herself to fall into the fantasy that what they'd shared in the past seven weeks wasn't a business deal or a bargain, but rather the solid basis for happily ever after.

Such a fool. She'd been such a fool.

Staring at the test window, she watched a bright blue plus sign appear. Her hands went to her stomach as joy fluttered through her. A baby. She closed her eyes as the thrill of her knowledge filled her.

Her sweet baby.

Chance's beloved baby.

In less than nine months, God willing, she would give birth to a healthy, beautiful baby. In less than nine months, she would be a mother.

Tears blurred her vision and she wasn't sure if they were tears of joy or tears of heartache. She swiped at them quickly, refusing to allow them to fall freely.

She knew Chance was waiting for her to come out of the bathroom. He was waiting to get the official results and she couldn't let him see how she really felt. Her pride would not allow it.

She tossed the test into the wastebasket, then left the bathroom and found Chance sitting at the table. She forced a smile and gave him a thumbs-up. "Mission accomplished," she said.

He stood, looking surprisingly ill-at-ease. "Well… that's great. Congratulations." He reached for her, and awkwardly they hugged. Almost immediately he stepped back from her, as if he didn't want to touch her.

Lana looked at her watch, trying to hide her heartache. "I'll probably have time to get packed up and get everything moved back to my apartment before dark."

"Lana, there's no need to rush things," he protested. He shoved his hands in his pockets, frowning thoughtfully. "You might as well stay here at the ranch until we get you in to see a doctor and get all the details squared away."

A reprieve, she thought. Despite the fact she knew it was foolish to put off the inevitable, she clutched on to the temporary suspension of complete and total heartbreak. "I'll call and make a doctor's appointment first thing in the morning," she replied.

He nodded and again an unusual awkwardness grew between them. Pulling his hands from his pockets, he eyed the bags of cabinet hardware they'd carried in. "I guess I'll get started on these cabinets," he said.

"If you don't mind, while you're working in here, I think I'll go visit for a little while with my mother." Lana hadn't seen her mom for a couple of weeks and suddenly found herself yearning for her mother's company.

"Sure. And take your time. We can just eat leftovers for dinner."

Moments later Lana was in her car and driving toward the Colton estate. "And take your time." Chance's parting words rang in her ears. Already it appeared he'd begun the separation process.

She would call the doctor in the morning and probably have an appointment by the end of the week and then she would have to figure out not only how to distance herself from Chance physically, but emotionally as well.

Within minutes the Colton home came into view. The enormous house perched high above the Pacific, with a terra-cotta-tiled roof and covered porches with thick columns. Impressive and quietly elegant, the house spoke of wealth and power.

The outbuildings she passed before reaching the circular drive of the main house were neat and attractive and told of a thriving, successful ranch.

She pulled around the circle drive, then parked and got out. There had been a time long ago when everyone used the front door, often greeted by the warm, gracious Meredith herself.

But those days were long gone and Lana walked around to the side door, where most of the deliveries were made.

Her mother answered the door. "Lana," she exclaimed, her dark eyes flashing with delight. "Come in, come in. I was just taking a little break with a cup of coffee."

The Colton kitchen was huge, yet Lana felt at home as her mother led her to the long table where the people who worked for the Coltons and sometimes the two youngest children ate their meals. "How about a cup of coffee?" Inez asked once Lana was settled at the table.

"No, thanks, Mama. I'm fine." To Lana's horror, she burst into tears.

Instantly Inez was at her side, her plump arms pulling Lana into an embrace. The familiar comfort of her mother's arms only made Lana cry harder.

"What is it, child?" Inez asked, a touch of fear radiating in her voice. "Are you hurt? Ill? Has something bad happened?"

Lana attempted to pull herself together, not wanting to frighten her mom. She moved out of Inez's embrace and swiped her tears with her fingertips. "Don't worry, it's nothing disastrous. I'm pregnant." The words blurted out of her with a renewed stream of tears.

Inez sat back in her chair and frowned. "But I thought this marriage to Chance wasn't a real marriage. I thought it was just to help him inherit the ranch."

Lana realized it was time to tell her mother the whole truth, the entire bargain she'd made with Chance. In halting words, she explained the situation and with each word her mother's frown etched deeper into her forehead.

"Oh, Lana, what would make you agree to such a thing?" Inez said when Lana had confessed all.

"I wanted to be a mother. I wanted a baby more than anything in the world."

"Then why are you sad? It seems you got exactly what you wanted."

Inez searched her daughter's face for a long moment, then sighed in obvious comprehension. "Ah, Lana, you played a dangerous game with your heart, and it appears it's a game you have lost."

Lana nodded miserably. She realized now she should have followed through on her original plan to be artificially inseminated. It was difficult to fall in love with a sterile needle.

"And so Chance has his ranch and you have your baby. What happens now?"

Lana shrugged. "Chance told me I can remain at the ranch until I see a doctor. Probably by the end of this week I'll be moving back to my apartment." Once again misery rose up inside her.

Inez's dark eyes shone with her disapproval. "You should have told me the truth from the very beginning. Perhaps I might have been able to talk you out of it."

"I thought I could handle it," Lana said softly.

"Honey, I saw the way you looked at Chance when you were nothing more than a child. That boy had your heart before you were old enough to understand the ways of love. Your father and I used to lie awake nights worrying because you loved him so, and you were so young and so vulnerable."

"I didn't realize I was still so vulnerable where he was concerned." Lana sighed. "I love him, Mama. I love him more than I ever thought possible."

"And how does Chance feel about you?"

Lana frowned. "I don't know," she finally admitted. "He's so difficult to read."

Inez nodded. "He was always closed off from every emotion other than his anger at his father. Tom Reilly scarred that boy deeply. He should have rejoined the army and left that boy to foster care instead of punishing Chance for his existence."

"I think someplace deep inside I hoped that my love could heal those scars," Lana admitted.

"You can't heal his scars, Lana. Only Chance can heal himself."

Lana knew her mother was right. She'd hoped somehow she could love Chance enough that he would be able to forget the painful memories the ranch house contained, that he would be able to open his heart to loving both that place...and ultimately her.

But at no time during the past seven weeks that they'd had together had he indicated any desire to change the terms of their original agreement.

Lana drew a deep breath and forced a smile of assurance to her lips. "I'll be all right."

"Well, of course you will," Inez agreed somberly. "You are a Ramirez and that means you're strong." Inez reached across the table and took Lana's hand in hers. "And you have a family that will stand behind you and support you as you raise your child." She squeezed Lana's hand reassuringly.

Although her mother's words couldn't begin to assuage the pain that ached deep inside Lana's heart, there was a certain comfort knowing she would really never be alone. As long as she had her parents and her sister, her child would be secure in love and devotion from the extended family.

Both women looked up as the kitchen door flew open and Meredith Colton stalked in. She was impeccably clad in an ice-blue Versace trouser suit that complemented her dramatically blond-streaked hair and her shapely figure.

She would have looked stunning if not for the angry press of her lips and the glittering hardness of her brown eyes.

"Inez, I must tell you the meal last night was completely unacceptable." Meredith didn't even acknowledge Lana's presence with a nod or a flicker of her eyes.

Inez stood, her expression one of studied dignity. "Could you be a little more specific, Mrs. Colton?"

Meredith's eyes narrowed and her nostrils flared slightly. "The chicken was overcooked, the vegetables were undercooked. The rolls were hard and the pastries were chewy. The centerpiece was wilted and there was a spot on the tablecloth. Is that specific enough for you?"

Lana felt her mother bristle beneath the imperious tone, but Inez merely nodded. "I'll see that tonight's dinner is perfect."

"Good, I absolutely refuse to put up with shoddy work." Meredith said, then turned on her heels and disappeared from the kitchen.

"That witch," Lana exclaimed angrily. "Why do you stay here, Mama? Why do you put up with her?"

A shadow of pain swept over Inez's dark eyes. "I stay because I remember the loving, warm woman she was before. And I stay for Joe and the rest of the family."

Lana's burst of anger seeped out of her. "I wonder what happened to make such a change in her. She used to be so kind, such a wonderful person."

Inez frowned. "I don't know what happened to her. Who knows? Disillusionment, broken dreams... Nobody can know what makes a body so miserable."

Later, as Lana drove back to the ranch, she thought about Meredith Colton and wondered what had happened to the woman she'd once been.

Somehow thoughts of Meredith and her unhappiness shifted to thoughts of Chance. If for some reason they would remain together, would Chance become a miserable, unhappy, hateful man, trapped into a place where he didn't want to be?

Was that what had happened to Chance's father? After Sarge Reilly's wife had died, had he longed to leave the ranch and rejoin the army only he couldn't because he had the responsibility of Chance?

It was ridiculous to speculate. If Chance had been willing to make a real go of their marriage, he would have already talked to her about that, he would have told her he loved her.

As she turned into the lane that led to the ranch, she felt the bittersweet warmth of a homecoming. After seven weeks, this place felt more like home than her apartment where she had lived for the past five years.

She knew that feeling of home came not from the structure and the land, but rather from Chance himself. Anywhere Chance was would feel like home to her.

A renewed wave of grief swept through her and she fought against it, knowing it was time for her to be strong and prepare to tell Chance Reilly goodbye.

Patsy Portman paced the lush carpeting in the master bedroom of the Colton estate. The cell phone in her pocket banged against her hip as she walked back and forth, her mind racing.

There was only one person who had the number to this particular cell phone…one man who she had been waiting to hear from for the past week. She was waiting to hear from the man who she had hired to kill Emily Blair Colton.

Silas Pike had called her the week before and told her he'd finally gotten a lead on Emily and was headed to a small town in Montana. Patsy had told him not to call her again until the deed was done.

What could be taking so long? How difficult could it be to get rid of one young woman who was all alone in a strange town?

Over the past ten years Patsy had done everything possible to make certain nobody could discover that she was not Meredith. The only loose end there had ever been was Emily.

Emily—a pain-in-the-ass nuisance who couldn't leave things alone.

Initially, immediately after the car wreck and the switch of identities, Emily had suffered nightmares and talked about two mommies. But she'd been young enough that nobody had paid much attention to her wild stories about that fateful day on the highway.

As she'd gotten older and her nightmares continued, along with flashes of memories of that day, Emily had become a direct threat to Patsy.

Emily could destroy the charade that Patsy had so carefully constructed. Emily could make sure that

Patsy was cast out from the lavish lifestyle as a Colton.

There was no way Patsy was going to let that happen. She loved being Meredith Colton with all the power and privileges that came with that title.

It didn't matter to her that her ''loving'' husband, Joe, had nothing to do with her, could barely stand looking at her. She didn't need him. All she wanted from him was his name and his money.

Through the years they had come to an agreement of sorts. He didn't bother her, preferring the company of his children, and she was allowed to live her own life. And she wasn't about to let that little twit Emily ruin it all for her.

Patsy still had things to do—like find her daughter, Jewel, the baby who'd been stolen from her mere hours after her birth.

She walked over to the expanse of windows that looked out over ragged cliffs that eventually led to the ocean below. Her hands closed into fists at her sides. She had worked hard to gain her place here, had plotted and planned so she would be in a position to steal Meredith's identity.

She should have pushed Emily over one of the balconies years ago. She should never have left the job to somebody else.

Silas ''Snake Eyes'' Pike. She'd met the man in a rough bar in L.A. while she was on her way to a stay at a spa in southern California. After making some subtle inquiries among some of the toughest, most disreputable-looking men she'd ever met, she'd decided Pike was the man to hire.

She'd found him surprisingly open about his background on the first night they had met. He'd told her about his abusive alcoholic father who had beaten his Native American mother to death, thrusting Silas into the foster care system where he'd quickly turned to a life of crime.

He'd bragged to her about his prison time served for car theft and armed robbery and boasted he'd made hits on all kinds of people from all walks of life.

Patsy hadn't cared about his past, she only wanted to know that he could deliver what he promised.

She'd told him what she wanted done, had paid him half of a promised fee, then had continued on to the spa, assured that her problem would be resolved within days.

But days had turned to weeks, and weeks into months and Silas Pike had yet to deliver. Patsy was beginning to think she'd hired Mr. Screwup instead of Mr. Snake Eyes.

She'd give him another week, then if she had to, she'd take a little trip to Montana and make certain Emily didn't have an opportunity to screw up the life Patsy had made for herself.

Eleven

"**M**rs. Reilly? The doctor will see you now."

Chance stood up as the nurse spoke to Lana, unsure what his role in this whole thing should be. Should he go back into the examining room with her? Should he stay out here in the waiting room?

Lana made the decision for him. She stood, shot him a nervous smile and told him she would return in a few minutes. Chance sat back down, trying to tamp down the nervous energy that ripped through him.

He was certain she was pregnant. She had all the signs, and the home test had indicated that she was, but it wouldn't seem real until a doctor gave them the official word.

It had been three days since she'd taken the test.

Three nights that they had slept in the same bed, but hadn't touched each other in any way. Chance had felt he might explode from wanting her, but he had fulfilled his duty and therefore felt he had no right to touch her, to make love to her anymore.

There had been a strained awkwardness between them. They were overly polite, like two strangers sharing intimate space but afraid of trespassing into each other's territory. Chance was almost sorry she'd taken the damn home pregnancy test. He almost wished things could go back to the way they had been.

He stood and began to pace, unable to sit while his head whirled with confusing thoughts. He didn't want to be married to Lana, and yet he enjoyed being married to Lana. He hated the ranch and yet had been reluctant to contact a Realtor and put the ball into motion to sell the place.

What was wrong with him? Why was he so conflicted in so many areas of his life when he'd always been so confident, so positive of the choices he had made in his life up until now?

"Mr. Reilly?" A nurse appeared at the door that led back to the examining rooms. "Could you come back with me, please?"

A flutter of fear swept through him. Was something wrong? Why would they want him back there? Fear crashed through him.

He hurriedly followed the nurse and was led to an examining room where Lana sat on the edge of a table, clad in a hospital gown that she somehow made look like a designer dress.

"What's wrong?" he asked worriedly when the nurse had left them alone in the room.

"I don't think anything is wrong. Dr. Hastings has already examined me and told me everything looks fine."

"So, it's official. You're pregnant," Chance said.

She nodded. "He said to expect a June baby." She smiled, a sweet dreamy expression on her face. "That's a wonderful month to have a baby, isn't it?"

A June baby. That meant she must have gotten pregnant on one of the first nights they'd been married. All the lovemaking they'd shared, all the intimacy they'd developed over the last seven weeks, hadn't been necessary after the first week or so.

Chance turned toward the door as Dr. Hastings walked back into the room. "Chance." The old doctor held a hand out. "Congratulations, my boy. It appears you're going to be a father."

Chance shook his hand and murmured his thanks. "So, everything seems normal?" he asked.

"As normal as Mother Nature makes things." Dr. Hastings turned to a cabinet and withdrew an instrument, then grinned at Chance. "I thought you might want to be here when we listen to the heartbeat." He motioned for Lana to lie down on the table, then flipped a switch and began to move the instrument across her lower tummy.

"Just a minute...just a minute...there!"

The room filled with the rhythmic sound of a heartbeat. Lana closed her eyes, a beatific smile on her lips, and Chance felt the hairs on the back of his neck raise in absolute wonder.

Dr. Hastings frowned and moved the instrument again. "What have we here?" he said as another heartbeat resounded. "I hear three distinct rhythms."

Lana's eyes flew open. "Three?" she said.

"Three?" Chance echoed in confusion.

Dr. Hastings removed the instrument and grinned at them. "Three," he repeated. "One of them is Lana's, the other two are babies."

"Two?" Lana whispered softly.

"Two?" Chance reached for the empty chair nearby and sank down as comprehension dawned. "Twins?"

"You got it," Dr. Hastings replied. "I guess double congratulations are in order."

Chance was numb with shock. He tried to focus on Hastings's words as he discussed a prescription for prenatal vitamins, the need for Lana to take it easy, and the importance of her eating right.

But focusing on the white-haired doctor's words was difficult when his mind was still working to accept the fact that Lana was going to have twins. Two babies. Twins.

"Sex is okay as long as you don't attempt to hang from a chandelier or something more adventurous," Dr. Hastings finished.

"I don't think you have to worry about anything like that," Lana replied with a pink stain to her cheeks.

Dr. Hastings laughed. "No, I didn't think so." He turned and looked at Chance. "Just take her home and take care of her. She mentioned some morning sickness. You might want to bring her a couple of crackers before she gets out of bed. Sometimes that helps. Other than that, just enjoy this magical time.''

A moment later Dr. Hastings left the room and Lana sat up, her gaze steady on Chance. "Do you have twins in your family?" she asked.

He shook his head. ''Not that I'm aware of. What about you?''

"No, I don't think so." She slid off the table and reached for her clothes.

"I'll just wait for you outside," Chance said, exiting the room before she could take off the gown. Since the day of her home pregnancy test, they had gone back to their privacy when dressing.

Chance returned to the waiting room, congratulated by everyone he passed on his way there. Everyone seemed so happy, as if twins were a wonderful blessing. He thought it was an absolute disaster.

How on earth did Lana intend to manage two babies? He'd heard that one could be quite difficult, crying at all times of the day and night, needing to be fed and changed, rocked and loved.

He clenched his hands. This hadn't been their bargain. He'd agreed to give her one baby, not two. Someplace in the back of his mind, he knew he was thinking irrationally. She hadn't intentionally gotten pregnant with twins.

Still, he couldn't help but worry and that hadn't been part of the deal, either. He had intended to walk away from her without a backward thought or concern. He wasn't supposed to be worried about her, afraid for her. She'd promised him no messy emotions, but at the moment his emotions were definitely a mess.

She returned to the waiting room and went directly to the receptionist desk to make another appointment, then together they walked out of the office building.

"Isn't it wonderful," she said, eyes shining brightly, as they walked down the sidewalk toward his car.

"*Wonderful* isn't exactly the word I would use."

She stopped walking and faced him, happiness lighting her features, making her so beautiful he ached with wanting her. "It's like a miracle," she said. "I was worried that any baby I had would be an only child. I knew after this deal with you was finished, I'd probably never have any more children. But now there will be a sibling—a twin." She tenderly touched her stomach.

"Lana, you aren't thinking clearly," he said, not wanting to upset her, but feeling as if she needed a dose of reality. "How on earth do you intend to manage two babies all alone?"

Her eyes were clear, her expression radiating that strength that he found so appealing. "Don't you worry, I'll manage these babies with love." She turned and continued down the sidewalk.

He followed behind her more slowly, wondering if along with pregnancy came delusional thinking. "Do you have your prescription for those vitamins?" he asked when they were back in his car.

"Yes, but I can pick them up later this week."

"Don't be ridiculous," he replied tersely. "We'll pick them up now." He backed out of the space where he'd been parked and headed down the street toward the drugstore. "Are you sure there aren't any twins in your family?" Although he hadn't intended it, there was a slightly accusatory tone to his voice.

"Why do I get the feeling that you're spoiling for a fight with me?"

He looked at her in surprise. "What makes you think that?"

"The expression on your face, the look in your eyes. Tell the truth. You're angry because there are two."

"That's crazy," he protested, even though he knew deep in his heart she was right.

"Yes, it is crazy." Her eyes flashed with fire and Chance realized it was the very first time he'd ever seen her angry. "I didn't plan this, but I consider it a blessing, a gift from God." She glared at him, as if daring him to say anything to the contrary. "Don't worry, Chance. Nothing has changed. Our agreement still stands."

Whatever he'd been about to say fled his mind as he realized he liked the fact that she was meeting him with anger, putting him in his place and standing up for herself and the babies she carried.

What he realized was he had been attempting to pick a fight with her, needing to release some of the energy that surged inside him.

But the truth was, he didn't want to fight, he wanted to hold her in his arms and make love to her sweetly and gently.

The past four nights of not making love to her had caused a pressure to build inside him, a pressure he didn't understand, one that frightened him just a little. He'd gone for weeks, sometimes months, between women before, so why should a mere four nights bother him?

He pulled up in front of the drugstore and turned to Lana. The midmorning sun shone through the car window, dousing her features with light.

She was beautiful, and again his mind filled with a vision of her four months from now, six months from now. Her belly would be rounded with the babies and he was certain she would look impossibly beautiful.

It was far too easy to visualize the two of them in bed at night, the skin of her protruding stomach soft beneath his fingers as he rubbed lotion on the growing mound to prevent stretch marks. It was far too easy to imagine sitting on the front porch and good-naturedly arguing over names for the babies.

Why did he still want her, when his job was done, his duty fulfilled? He could smell the scent of her, that subtle floral fragrance that made his blood rush too fast inside his veins.

He felt the need for some space from her, the need to escape his thoughts. He didn't want to think about babies and names, or Lana. "Do you have the prescription?"

She nodded and unclasped her seat belt.

"You don't have to get out," he said. "I'll run in and get it."

She hesitated a moment, then acquiesced and pulled the prescription from her purse.

"Lana," he began thoughtfully. "You know

there's really no reason for you to leave the ranch until it's sold.''

"There's really no point in me remaining there,'' she countered, her voice soft, yet emotionless.

"I don't want you in your apartment by yourself while you're having morning sickness. You shouldn't be alone right now.''

"Then I'll stay until the ranch is sold,'' she agreed after a moment of hesitation.

"Good. I'll be right back,'' he said and quickly made his escape.

Inside the drugstore, Chance handed the prescription to the druggist, then wandered the aisles while he waited for the prescription to be filled.

His entire world had been shaken up by the information that Lana was carrying twins and he knew he still hadn't fully assessed the ramifications of the news.

"Don't worry, Chance. Nothing has changed. Our agreement still stands.'' Lana's words whirled around and around in his head.

It was obvious she was thrilled with the whole development. She didn't seem to have any doubts about her capacity to single-handedly parent two babies.

She apparently hadn't thought about the fact that few men were willing to take on a divorcee with a child, and even fewer men would be willing to take on a divorcee with two children. By agreeing to this arrangement he might be responsible for Lana spending the rest of her life alone.

And she certainly hadn't indicated in any way that she would like it if he stuck around. And why should she want him to stick around? He was a loser, a nothing, a man who wasn't a keeper.

The best thing he could do for her was walk away. Walk away before he ruined her life and the lives of her babies.

As the druggist called his name, he walked back to the counter and paid for the prescription. At the same time he came to a decision. First thing in the morning he would go to one of the Realtors in town and put the ranch on the market. It was time.

Running. Running. Emily tore through brush, whipped around trees, and always, always when she looked behind her Snake Eyes Pike was there. She knew if she ran fast enough, safety lay in the small cottage just ahead. Toby would be there to protect her.

The wind that surrounded her as she ran was cold, and the tree branches reached out with gnarled limbs as if to impede her forward progress. Her breaths came in short gasps as she struggled to stay ahead of the danger behind.

She yelled triumphantly as she reached the cottage and flung open the front door. "Toby!" she called, knowing the handsome lawman would let nobody harm her.

Toby cared about her. He was strong and good, and he wouldn't let Snake Eyes get her. He'd protect her. He'd save her.

Then she saw him. Toby. Dead on the floor in front of her. The front of his shirt was soaked with his blood and to her horror he sat up, eyes staring at her accusingly. "This is all your fault," he said.

Emily jerked awake and for a moment sheer panic coursed through her before she realized the horrid images had been part of a dream.

She was no longer in the woods. She was no longer even in Wyoming. But Toby was still dead. Tears oozed down her cheeks as grief ripped through Emily. Toby was dead and it was all her fault.

If only she hadn't encouraged the handsome lawman's friendship, if only she had warned him by telling him the truth about herself. If only... if only. Guilt coupled with her grief, momentarily overwhelming her. It would have been better if Snake Eyes Pike had killed her instead of shooting the sweet, loving, protective Toby.

She wept until there were no tears left to fall, until she felt as if every drop of moisture had been cried from her body. Finally, she sat up and thought back over the past three days.

After Toby had died and she had run out of the little cottage, she'd made her way to the highway, but had been too afraid to step out of the brush and flag down a car. Her anguish over Toby had been shoved deep inside, her instinct for survival had been first and foremost in her mind.

It wasn't until the early dawn that she finally got up her nerve to leave the safety of the brush and venture out closer to the highway. She knew she couldn't go to Wyatt, or back to Montana, but she had to run, to escape the nightmare. She'd flagged down an eighteen-wheeler and had hitched a ride to the nearest airport, where she'd managed to buy a ticket to Washington D.C.

She'd called her eldest brother, Rand, from the D.C. airport, sobbing into the phone, and within an hour, she was in his car and headed for his luxury town house.

There, she was introduced to his new wife, Lucy, and his stepson, a precocious, five-year-old Max. After Max was in bed that evening, Emily told Rand and Lucy what had happened with Snake Eyes Pike and Toby.

Even though they tried to comfort her, assuring her that none of it was her fault and they were just grateful she was safe, there was no solace in their words.

Emily's despair was so abysmal, she knew no words would ever, could ever make her feel better. A man had died because of her, and a part of her had died along with him.

Wearily, despite her long nap, she pulled herself out of bed and into the adjoining bathroom. She stared at her reflection in the mirror, wondering how it was possible that she looked the same as she had before the tragedy.

Why hadn't her long mane of chestnut-red hair turned white with the fright of the trauma? Why hadn't her blue eyes dulled from the profound ache in her heart? Why did she still look so normal when she now had the burden of a man's death wrapped like a thousand-pound weight around her heart?

Tears once again welled up inside her and she tried to shove them aside. She couldn't stop crying. She'd been here almost two days and still she couldn't stop the tears that seemed to have an inexhaustible source.

Swiping at her cheeks, she drew a deep breath in an attempt to steady her chaotic emotions. She didn't want to frighten little Max with her continuous crying.

She left the bathroom and headed for the kitchen and there she found Rand, Lucy and Max preparing for the evening meal.

"Emily!" Lucy immediately rushed to her side. "You're just in time for dinner. We didn't know whether to wake you or let you nap."

Emily smiled at the pretty woman. Although they'd only known each other a brief time, Emily already felt the warmth of friendship and a familial connection. "Thanks. I think I'm all napped out."

"Come and sit," Rand said and pointed to the chair next to Max.

"I was quiet as a mouse while you were napping," Max observed soberly.

Emily smiled at the little boy. He was a doll, with his straight, dark brown hair, his big blue eyes and the smattering of freckles across the bridge of his nose. The eyeglasses he wore somehow only added to his appeal. "And I truly appreciate your thoughtfulness," she said.

Max nodded with a grown-up air. It had taken Emily only minutes with the little boy to realize he was quite bright and seemed far older than he really was.

"How are you doing?" Rand asked, his blue eyes boring into hers.

"I'm all right," she replied, her voice shakier than

she would have liked and her eyes once again burning with the press of tears.

Rand covered her hand with his. "We'll get through this," he said firmly. "You just wait and see. Everything is going to be just fine."

"Just fine and dandy," Max added and they all laughed.

As they ate, Emily tried not to think about Toby, but thoughts of him kept intruding. Had somebody found him? What a devastating thing his death would be for his brother, Josh.

Emily knew that Toby and Josh's mother had died when Toby was young and their father had been an alcoholic. Josh had raised his younger brother and the two had been extremely close. Did he even know yet that the brother he'd raised, the brother he loved, was dead?

"I spoke to the authorities in Keyhole," Rand said, almost as if he'd read Emily's thoughts. "You don't have to worry about Silas Pike any longer. He was found in the woods outside the cottage and is now in the jail infirmary recovering from a leg wound."

Lucy cleared her throat, as if to remind Rand that Max was at the table, listening to each and every word of the conversation.

Emily knew Rand meant the words to be comforting, but all she could think about was how unfair it was that Silas Pike would recover, and sweet, gentle Toby would not.

"Has Pike said anything?" she asked, wondering if he'd admitted that he'd been hired to kill her.

Rand shook his head. "So far, the man isn't saying

a word, but he's going to be charged with homicide and I imagine it won't be long before he's singing to anyone who might listen.''

Emily nodded and returned her focus to her food, although she had no appetite. She couldn't eat. Her heart was so heavy in her chest, she felt that if she took a bite and tried to swallow she might be violently ill.

They had finished eating and Emily had just helped Lucy with the dishes when the phone rang. Rand answered it in his office, then brought the receiver to Emily.

"It's Mother," he said as he gave her the phone.

Emily clutched the receiver to her ear. "Mama?"

"Sparrow." The familiar voice and the childhood nickname released the tears Emily had been trying so desperately to hold back.

"Mama," she sobbed, wishing Meredith was here to hold her, to somehow take away the pain as only a mother could.

"Rand told me what happened and I am so glad you weren't hurt," Meredith said.

"But, Toby…" Again Emily was overwhelmed with weeping.

"It's going to be all right, my precious Sparrow. I'm going to fly there tomorrow, then together we're all going to go home. Back to the ranch, back where we all belong."

Emily clutched at her mother's words, hoping, praying it was as easy as her mother had made it sound. Back to the ranch. Home.

* * *

Meredith replaced the receiver and turned to look at Dr. Wilkes. "And so, I'll be leaving for Washington D.C. first thing in the morning."

Martha Wilkes smiled, her beautiful ebony features radiating strength. "How do you feel about going back to Prosperino and your family?"

"Scared to death," Meredith admitted. She was frightened, frightened of going back and facing the twin sister who had so wronged her and she was frightened of trying to pick up the pieces of a life in which she'd been ten years absent. "I still don't have all my memories, but I can't put this off any longer."

"Because of what happened to Emily?" Dr. Wilkes asked. Meredith had shared with the psychiatrist the events that had happened in Keyhole.

Meredith nodded, her heart aching for the child who had been left behind on the day of the accident so long ago, a child who had grown into a young woman and had just suffered an enormous trauma. "She needs me now. Not next week, not next month, but right now. Besides, it's time." Meredith lifted her chin. "It's time I go back to Prosperino and reclaim what is mine."

Dr. Wilkes reached out and grabbed Meredith's hands. "You'll be fine, Meredith. I have to tell you, it's been a pleasure knowing you and working with you. You are one of the strongest women I've ever met and I've come not only to like you, but to respect you."

Tears burned at Meredith's eyes as she squeezed Martha's hands. "Thank you. I don't know what I would have done without you."

Martha smiled. "You would have survived, and eventually you would have come to the place where you are now. Go home and take back what was stolen from you. Embrace the family who might have momentarily left your mind, but never left your heart. And stay in touch."

"I will," Meredith promised as she released the doctor's hands. "I'll call and let you know how things are going." Impulsively, she threw her arms around the woman who had been instrumental in returning her identity to her. "Thank you, Dr. Wilkes," she said, then quickly left the office before her tears could fall.

As Meredith drove away from the office that had become like a second home to her, her mind whirled with the enormity of what lay ahead.

Every day another piece of her memory returned, some of those pieces happy, some of them sad. She'd remembered the joy of her first child's birth, remembered the feeling of intense love that had swept through her when Rand was first placed in her arms. And she'd wept when the memory of her son Michael's death had resurfaced. Michael, one of twin boys, had been killed by a drunk driver when he'd been riding his bicycle.

There was only one deep blank place in Meredith's memory. She could remember the feel of her husband's arms around her. Her mind had retrieved the gentleness of his touches and the laughter they had often shared. But Joe's face remained a blank. No matter how hard she tried, she couldn't remember her husband's appearance. And that worried her.

Was there some reason why his facial features remained elusive to her? What had Patsy managed to do to the marriage Meredith had shared with Joe?

If only she had told Joe years ago about Patsy. Patsy's life had been troubled for years. Her past included a child born out of wedlock and a second-degree murder conviction for killing the baby's father in a scuffle.

When Meredith had first met Joe Colton, she'd been too ashamed to tell him about her sister. Besides, Meredith had promised her mother she would never tell anyone about Patsy and the scandal of her conviction.

Still, as Meredith and Joe grew closer, Meredith longed to tell the truth to the man she loved, but as the years passed and the timing never seemed right, the secret got more difficult to confess. She knew now that if she had told Joe about Patsy, Patsy would have never been able to steal Meredith's life.

She pulled her car in front of her house. Tonight would be the last night she would sleep in this place. Tomorrow night she would be at Rand's in Washington D.C. and after that, God willing, she would finally, truly be home.

Twelve

Lana watched from the window as Chance and Lester Pierce from Prosperino Realty Company walked around the corral area. She could tell by the way Lester was shaking his head enthusiastically that he was impressed with the work that had been done around the place and was already anticipating a quick sale and a big commission.

She turned away from the window, unable to watch while Chance made the arrangements to sell her dream, to irrevocably break her heart.

Sinking down at the table, she tried not to think about how solicitous Chance had been the night before and all that morning.

He'd greeted her in bed with a saucer full of crackers, instructing her to eat several before attempting to move. She'd done just that and had been pleasantly surprised that the morning sickness passed more quickly than usual.

Since getting out of bed, Chance had insisted she sit and relax while he threw a load of laundry into the washer, then took out a pound of hamburger from the freezer for supper that evening.

"Chance, I'm pregnant, not terminally ill," she'd protested.

"You're pregnant with twins, and the doctor said he didn't want you stressed or to overdo."

"I don't intend to overdo," she protested, although she said nothing about being somewhat stressed. She couldn't help but be stressed when she thought of Chance selling the ranch, leaving Prosperino and dashing any lingering hope she might entertain of their marriage becoming a lasting one.

Still, for the remainder of the afternoon, Chance had treated her like an invalid, waiting on her hand and foot and doing the household chores she normally did. And every minute of the afternoon had radiated with the simmering tension that existed between them.

She wasn't sure if the tension was because Chance was still upset that she was having twins or if it had its source somewhere else.

She knew she felt edgy and slightly out of sorts. She knew it was because she desperately wanted Chance to make love to her again, she desperately wanted to be held in his arms, taste his mouth against hers and for just a moment feel her love for him explode in her heart.

It had almost been a relief when Lester had shown up right after supper for a tour of the place. Lana cleared off the dishes, washed them and put them away, then sat at the table and sipped a glass of orange juice.

She knew it had been pure madness to agree to remain here until the ranch sold. The place would probably sell within a week or two. Or, it was possible it might take months for the right buyer to come along.

Months that she could spend here with Chance, months in which she could simply fall more and more in love with him, making their final separation all that much more painful.

She should have moved back to her apartment the first morning she'd felt sick and had suspected it was morning sickness. But she didn't have the strength to deny herself one minute, one hour, one day of time with Chance.

And there was still a small flame of hope alive inside her, a tiny kernel of hope that he just might love her back and decide to stay here and help her raise his babies.

She stood as Chance and Lester came in through the back door. "I told you to leave the dishes," Chance said. "I would have taken care of them."

"I'm fine, Chance." She forced a smile of greeting to Lester. She liked the man fine, but it was difficult to be friendly to a man who intended to take away your dream. "Nice to see you, Lester."

"And you." Lester returned her smile. "And I understand congratulations are in order. Chance told me you're adding to your family.''

Adding two and subtracting one, Lana thought, then shoved the painful thought aside. ''Yes, we're very excited.''

''Let me show you the house,'' Chance said, his voice a gruff command. As he led Lester out of the kitchen, Lana heard him explaining that there were a few things that would need to be done to the house, but that Chance didn't intend to do them.

She knew he was talking about the hole in the Shcetrock in the spare bedroom and the broken bathroom door lock. He refused to fix them because they represented his childhood pain, his anger at his father. And she believed that as long as his heart was filled with that unresolved anger, he would never fully open himself up to love.

Yet, she knew it was possible she was kidding herself, that Chance's heart would open to love with the right woman, and Lana simply wasn't the woman for him.

But, oh, how he felt like the man for her. She had grown to love the way he looked first thing in the morning, with his gold-streaked brown hair tousled from sleep and his cheeks dusky with a night's whisker growth.

She adored the way his beautiful green eyes transmitted his emotions, lightening when he laughed, and deepening when he was intense and thoughtful.

She loved him, but she wasn't sure she understood him. There were many evenings when they sat side-by-side on the front porch and she'd feel sweet contentment radiating from him. There were many nights, before the pregnancy test, when he'd held her in his arms and she'd felt love emanating from him and thundering in his heartbeat.

Or was she only imagining those emotions? Was the contentment she thought she felt from him actually a wistfulness for his life back in the midwest? Was the love she sometimes felt wafting from him actually the simple passion of a virile man for any woman?

She stood as Lester and Chance returned to the kitchen. "It's a great place," Lester said enthusiastically. "I'm sure it will sell quickly. I'll get it listed first thing in the morning for the price we discussed and I've got a For Sale sign in my car, so we'll get it up before I leave."

Chance nodded, his expression unreadable.

"Could you and Lana come into the office first thing in the morning and sign the realty contract?"

Chance looked at Lana. She nodded and tried to ignore the dull ache in her heart. "That will be fine," Chance said to Lester. "But let's make it early afternoon instead of first thing in the morning."

A surge of love filled Lana as she realized he was making the appointment in the afternoon in deference to her. He knew that lately mornings were difficult for her.

As Lester and Chance walked out to Lester's car, Lana made half a pot of coffee, knowing Chance liked to end the day by sitting on the porch and sipping a cup of coffee.

The sound of Lester's car pulling out of the driveway came just as the coffee finished brewing. Lana pulled on a lightweight sweater, then poured Chance a cup of coffee and left the house.

The first thing that struck her eyes when she reached the door was the large For Sale sign in the front yard. The significance of all that the sign implied hit her like a slap in the face, an arrow in the heart.

Chance sat in the chair where he usually sat, a thoughtful expression on his handsome face. He looked up as she stepped out on the porch. Seeing the coffee mug in her hand, he jumped up to help her.

"Sit down," she commanded as she handed him the mug. "I can manage getting my—you a cup of coffee without needing help." She'd been about to say "my husband," but she had to stop thinking of Chance as her husband. It wouldn't be long now and he'd be out of her life.

It was time she started removing him from her mind—and attempted to release him from her heart.

"You're nothing, boy. You never were worth anything and you'll always be nothing." Sarge Reilly glared at his son.

As always, Chance knew he was dreaming, but he couldn't pull himself out of the nightmare, nor could he escape the intense emotional pain that racked him as his father berated him.

Simply words, he told himself, but the power of those words battered him like fists and again he swallowed in an attempt to contain the tears that pressed perilously close to the surface.

"Run, boy. Sell this place and run as far and as fast as you can. That woman and those babies will be better off without you. They don't need a loser in their lives."

Sarge's words pierced him like bullets. He needed to escape, to run, but when he turned, Lana stood there, blocking his path.

She opened her arms to him, and he knew in her arms was his salvation. But as he tried to go to her, his father grabbed him from behind, making it impossible.

"Chance!"

With a start, he tumbled from his dream world and into reality. Moonlight streaked into the windows, filling the bedroom with enough light that he could see Lana gazing at him, a worried crinkle in the center of her forehead.

"Are you all right? You were crying out."

His first impulse was to say that he was fine, that it was just a dumb dream. But that wasn't the truth, and the empty platitude didn't make it to his lips.

"No, I'm not all right." He sat up and raked his fingers through his hair, aware that his heart still beat the accelerated rhythm of confrontation with his father. "It was a nightmare."

She sat up and touched his arm lightly. "Is there anything I can do?" she asked, her eyes luminous and achingly earnest.

His need for her exploded inside him, shooting heat through his veins and setting his nerve endings aflame. He had not touched her since the day she'd taken her pregnancy test, but now he could not deny the need that suffused him.

He said nothing, but instead wrapped his arms around her and claimed her mouth with his. He half expected a protest to rise to her lips. Instead, she simply kissed him back.

Together they fell back on the bed, arms wrapped around each other and lips locked feverishly. Neither spoke as the kiss deepened and heartbeats raced.

Chance wanted to make love to her and he could tell by the heat of her kiss, by the way her hands stroked over his shoulders, across his back, that she wanted him, too.

There was no longer any bargain to fulfill, no baby to make, there was absolutely no reason for them to make love except the incredible desire to hold her in his arms, feel her body next to his, lose himself in her embrace.

What was wondrous and amazing was he felt the same emotions radiating from her. She clung to him as if her hunger was as great as his. He realized it was more than physical hunger that drove them together, it was a need to connect on a deeper level than just with mere bodies. It was a desire to touch the light of her soul, knowing it would banish the darkness in his.

With a whisper and a sigh, her nightgown seemed to melt away, leaving her warm and pliant in his arms. There was no urgency between them, no pressure to hurry. Rather he wanted each touch, every caress to linger for an eternity.

As he swept his hand across her lower abdomen,

he thought he felt a subtle fullness that hadn't been there before. Babies. Twin babies.

His babies.

Awe swept through him as for the first time since the doctor's visit the fact that Lana was carrying his twins sank in. A part of him, a part of her, growing inside her...their babies.

The skin across her stomach was silky smooth, and he wondered how long it would be before a hand on her belly might feel the kick of a tiny foot, or the jab of a little elbow.

As he claimed Lana's lips again, all thoughts of babies fled as his mind, his senses, his very being, were filled with her.

They made love slowly, with a tenderness he'd never known before. He could feel her heartbeat as he possessed her, a steady, rapid beating that echoed comfortably deep inside him.

Afterward, they remained locked in an embrace, neither speaking as they waited for heartbeats to slow and breathing to resume a more normal pace.

Within minutes he knew Lana had fallen back to sleep. Her light breaths were warm against the side of his neck, and one of her arms was flung across his chest.

He turned to gaze at her, grateful for the moonlight that allowed him to see her features as she slept. She had never looked more beautiful than she did at this moment, with her hair tousled and her cheeks still colored from their exertions. Her lips were slightly swollen and her eyes moved rapidly behind the lids.

He wondered if she was dreaming. If she was, he

hoped she had happy dreams. He frowned. Soon she would have no time to dream, she'd barely find time to sleep. Two babies.

He eased away from her and got out of bed, suddenly too restless to sleep. He grabbed a pair of jeans and a shirt, then left the bedroom.

He dressed quickly then stepped out the front door, where the moon not only lit the land with a silvery glow, but also played on the real estate sign in the middle of the front yard.

Easing down on one of the chairs on the porch, Chance fought to sort out the emotions that raged through him. He'd thought he knew what he wanted from life, what he intended to get out of life, but now all his preconceived wants seemed selfish and shallow.

That woman and those babies don't need a loser in their lives. Sarge's words from Chance's nightmare played and replayed in his mind.

But they did need somebody, and Chance knew nobody else was going to step in. All his life, he'd made his decisions to prove that Sarge was wrong about him. Yet, the decisions he'd made had simply proven how right Sarge had been.

Chance had spent his life running from commitments, escaping any real responsibility. It had always been easier to run than to take the risk of disappointing anyone or proving without a doubt that his father had been right about him and he was a loser.

Again his mind filled with thoughts of Lana, who had transformed the ranch house into a home. Lana, who had rubbed the sore muscles of his back without him asking, who had drawn him a hot bath after a particularly grueling day.

Since the moment they had gotten married, Lana had seemed to work extra hard to make Chance's life happy. She laughed at his stupid jokes, didn't complain when he left his dirty clothes in the middle of the bathroom floor. She seemed to sense when he needed a touch of her hand, a smile of encouragement or simply an understanding silence.

And now she needed him.

He leaned back in the chair and thought of how sick Lana had been each morning, and how her energy level had lowered over the past couple of days. She needed him now, and he knew when the babies were born she would need him even more.

When he'd made the bargain with her, he'd believed it would be easy to walk away. He'd never know now if he would have been able to walk away from her if she'd been pregnant with one baby.

He certainly hadn't counted on twins. Neither had she. But the fact that there were two babies negated their original agreement.

Those babies needed a real home, with a father and a mother present. Lana needed a husband, a companion to help with feeding and bathing, changing and rocking the babies. She needed him.

If he walked away now, he would be living up to his father's expectations. Maybe it was time he tried to exceed everyone's expectations, including his own.

Decision made, he stood and walked off the porch. In the light of the silvery moonshine, he hurried across the grass to where the real estate sign stood.

Grabbing it with both hands, he tugged it out of the ground and carried it to the barn. He set it inside, then returned to the porch and looked around one last time.

This ranch, which had been the place of Chance's misery for years, would now be his legacy of love to his children. A surge of emotions welled up inside him.

Tomorrow he'd go to town and order not one, but two of those canopied cribs she'd seen in the store. His heart swelled as he thought of her happiness when she saw the two cribs in the spare room.

Silently, he went into the house, undressed, then slid back in bed beside Lana, who still slept soundly. He closed his eyes, his heart at peace.

For the first time in his life he felt as if he'd made the right decision. He was not going to sell the ranch. He was not going to run away.

He would stay, because Lana needed him.

Meredith stood at the guest bedroom window in Rand's town house, staring out at the darkness of the night. Tomorrow. The thought of the day to come held both the promise of incredible joy and the possibility of enormous heartache.

What havoc had Patsy wrought in the life she had stolen? The family that had been so important to Meredith—had Patsy managed to destroy it?

A slight moan broke the silence and Meredith turned away from the window and gazed at Emily, who restlessly slept in the bed nearby.

Although Rand's town home had enough bedrooms for Emily and Meredith to have had their own for the night, Emily had insisted she wanted to sleep in Meredith's room.

Meredith's heart expanded as she gazed at the young woman with the moonlight shining on her face. Her little Sparrow. Of all the foster children she and Joe had taken in, Emily had been special...so special she and Joe had adopted her.

But Emily wasn't little anymore. Rather she was a beautiful woman carrying a heart full of anguish. Since Meredith's arrival here and after hearing the story about Toby and Snake Eyes Pike, she'd been worried sick about her daughter.

The light in Emily's beautiful blue eyes had been extinguished, as if a piece of her had died along with the hero lawman.

"Patsy, how could you have done something like this?" Meredith whispered softly. Her heart ached for her troubled sister, yet at the same time she raged for all the evil that Patsy had spawned.

Meredith leaned her forehead against the window, the glass cool with the late October air. And why with almost all of her memories returned to her, did she still have blank spaces where Joe was concerned?

Was it possible he wasn't the man who had haunted her when she had positively no memories at all? At that time, she'd dreamed of a man's arms around her, holding her close. She'd felt a sense of deep security, a wave of belonging and had ached to be with that man again.

Had it been Joe that she had dreamed about? Or had those dreams merely been the fantasies of a lonely, unloved woman?

Tomorrow. She shivered, both anxious and afraid to discover what the day would bring.

Thirteen

    "**W**e need to talk," Chance said to Lana the next morning when she came into the kitchen.

She sank down at the table, her cheeks instantly warming as she thought of their middle-of-the-night lovemaking. Was that what he wanted to discuss? Did he intend to make up some excuse? Offer some explanation that had nothing to do with love or desire? If he did, she thought her heart would break in two.

"About what?" She hoped he couldn't read any of her thoughts in her expression as she gazed at him.

He sank onto the chair next to hers. "Late last night I went out and took down the For Sale sign. I put it in the barn."

She stared at him in surprise. "I—I don't understand."

"I'm not selling."

Her heart thundered against her ribs and hope spilled shining rays of light through her. She tried to ignore it, not wanting to second-guess his intentions and be disappointed. "Then, what are you going to do?" she asked softly.

His gaze held hers, his eyes as green as sweet pastures, as warm as spring sunshine. "I'm going to renege on our bargain."

"Renege?" Her head swam as her heartbeat accelerated to what felt like a feverish pace.

"I'm not selling, Lana. I'm not leaving you and the babies."

The hope that she'd been afraid to release fluttered through her, as rich, as wondrous as the new lives inside her. "But what about your life back in the Midwest? What about your job?"

"My life is here." He stood and walked over to the window and stared out. "And my work is here." He turned back to face her. "We'll build this ranch into something magnificent for the twins. We'll make this place the home that it never was for me."

He walked back to the table and once again sat next to her. Taking her hands in his, his expression was nakedly earnest. "When we made our agreement, we didn't know you'd get pregnant with twins. I can't walk away now. What do you say, Lana? Build a life here with me. You need me, and those babies are going to need me."

His words should have sent joy winging through her. This was what she had hoped for, what she had prayed would happen. She waited for the joy to suffuse her, but it didn't. What did sweep through her was confusion and a strange sense of disappointment.

She broke eye contact with him and instead stared down at the tabletop, trying to discern the emotions that roared through her. "I don't know, Chance. I—I need to think about it. I need a little time." She looked at him again.

He nodded and released her hands. "I know I sort of sprung this on you out of nowhere and I know it isn't what we initially agreed upon." He swept a hand through his hair and leaned back in the chair. "But we're good together, aren't we? We could make a good life here together for the kids."

"Yes, we're good together," she conceded, a deep pain growing in her heart.

Chance stood once again. "I've got some errands to run in town. Why don't we talk when I get back? That will give you a little time to think."

She nodded and stood as well and walked with him to the front door. "While you're out, would you pick up some candy for trick-or-treaters?"

"That's right, that's tomorrow, isn't it?"

"I don't know how many children you get out here, but I thought we'd better be prepared," she said.

"I'll pick some up." His gaze on her was once again intense, somber. He reached out and touched her cheek with his index finger. "You need me, Lana. Let me be there for you." With these final words, he turned and left her standing at the door.

Lana watched until his sports car had disappeared from view, then she went into the living room and sank down on the sofa.

Chance was going to stay. He wanted to build a life with her and their children. So, where was her joy? Why wasn't she happy?

She replayed his words over and over again in her mind, and as she did, she recognized the source of her disappointment.

Chance had talked of *her* need for him, and the babies' need, but he hadn't said a word about *his* need for her. He hadn't said a word about loving her.

If she were only carrying one baby, would he be making the same decision? Until the moment they had discovered she was carrying twins, he'd made no indication he intended to stay at the ranch and make a go of their marriage.

His decision had been made through duty and responsibility, not because of love. And as much as she loved him, as much as she desired to build a life with him, she would not remain in this marriage.

In fact, the need to escape suddenly consumed her. If she remained here, when Chance returned he would talk her into staying. She had no strength where he was concerned and it would be far too easy to give in to him.

However, she knew what the consequences would be. Eventually Chance would become resentful. He would feel trapped in a situation he'd professed he didn't want. And as his unhappiness grew, perhaps he would become more like his father...unable to contain his bitterness.

Lana pulled herself up and off the sofa. She'd been a fool to remain here as long as she had. She should have left when she'd initially suspected she was pregnant.

The thought of leaving now ripped a hole inside her, but she knew she had no other choice. Going into the bedroom, she tried to keep her heart, her mind empty. She couldn't think about what she was doing, couldn't dwell on it or she would lose herself in tears, lose the courage she needed to do the right thing.

It didn't take her long to pack a suitcase with her most immediate needs. She gathered her toiletries and makeup from the bathroom, fighting against the tears that burned her eyes. She worked quickly, unsure how long Chance would be gone and knowing it was imperative that she be gone by the time he returned home.

Before Chance sold the place, she'd make arrangements to get the rest of her things. She was certain that he would sell when he discovered she didn't intend to stay married to him. Although he might initially protest her decision, deep inside she was certain he would be relieved.

Chance was a good man and he'd made the offer to be a real husband to her, a real father to their children because of his moral caliber. But Lana loved him too much to allow him to sacrifice his life for her.

She wrote a brief note and propped it up on the kitchen table, unable to walk away without a word of explanation.

It was time to say goodbye. Past time.

She held in her tears until she had her car packed and walked to the barn for the For Sale sign that

Chance had taken down the night before. As she entered the barn, the tears could no longer be contained.

Half-blinded by blurry tears, she grabbed the sign and carried it back to the front yard. She shoved it into the ground and for a moment leaned against it, overwhelmed by grief.

She allowed herself only a few minutes to weep, then drove away from the ranch.

It was over. Finished.

There was no happily-ever-after for her and Chance. Her prayers had fallen on deaf ears, for she had prayed, not for Chance to stay, but rather for Chance to love her.

As she drove away, Lana refused to look in her rearview mirror. She didn't want a last look at the home where she'd been introduced to passion, where she had dreamed of raising children and putting down roots.

She didn't want a last look at the place that had come to represent the man she loved.

It had been a stupid bargain that they'd made. Her mother had been right, she'd played a game with her heart and she'd lost.

She'd promised him no messy emotions when the time came to part and that was exactly what she would give him. He would never know the depth of her despair, never be allowed to see her overwhelming love for him.

She'd go back to her apartment and build a home there for herself and her two children. And perhaps, if fate were kind, in time she would forget both the boy she had fallen in love with so many years ago and the man he'd become. The man who had stolen her heart.

Chance never sang when he was happy. Unlike his mother, who had either not known or hadn't cared that she was tone-deaf, he knew he couldn't carry a tune. Instead, when he was happy, he whistled.

His whistling filled the car as he drove back toward the ranch. He'd accomplished a lot in the two hours he'd spent in town. He'd spoken with Lester Pierce and pulled his ranch off the market, then he'd gone into the baby store and ordered two of the fancy cribs that Lana had liked.

He'd finally ended up in the local discount store where he bought several bags of candy and watched as a couple of kids tried to decide which Halloween costume to buy.

As he'd watched the kids sort through colorful wigs and witches' hats, he'd realized that in a couple of years, he and Lana would be buying costumes for their own children.

Would they have two girls…two fairy princesses? Or two rough-and-tumble boys? Or perhaps one of each? At some point between the time the doctor had told Chance about the twins and now, Chance had embraced the babies to his heart.

He would not be a father like Sarge. He had nothing but love in his heart for the babies Lana carried, and he knew he could never be the kind of cruel, difficult man that Sarge had been.

For years he'd worried that the apple didn't fall far from the tree, that too many pieces of his father resided inside him for him to ever be a loving, caring parent.

Chance's fears had even come out in his dreams, when he'd dreamed of his father telling him that he wasn't dead, but would always live inside Chance's heart and soul.

Now, with the love for his children sweeping through him, filling his heart, Chance knew that somehow his father had been truly laid to rest.

Chance wasn't his father, and he had the memory of his mother's love, her gentle nature and her cheerful laughter inside his heart. He knew he was going to be a wonderful father, and this knowledge filled him with a joy he'd never experienced before.

He pulled into the lane that would take him home, a sense of pride rising up as he saw the house and the outbuildings in the distance. The place looked well-kept, loved.

Funny, how he'd told himself he hated this place, how he'd somehow believed that the house, the barn, the very land itself was tainted with his father's rage.

Those nights of sitting on the front porch with Lana had renewed his love for this place. Watching the sun set each evening, enjoying good conversation, he'd remembered all the hopes and dreams he'd once entertained.

He would never have the family he'd wanted with his father. It was far too late for the two of them to bond, to build something good and worthwhile, but Chance could build those dreams, those hopes with Lana.

The first thing he'd do when he got home was fix

the bathroom door lock and the Sheetrock in the spare bedroom. It was time—past time—to let go of the past. He no longer saw it as fixing his father's messes, but rather as healing his own wounds and getting on with the rest of his life.

Pulling into the driveway, he frowned as he saw the For Sale sign in the yard. How had that gotten back up? Was it possible somebody else from the realty company had been out while he was gone and put a new sign up?

He parked, grabbed his plastic shopping bag of candy and hurried into the house. "Lana?" he called as he stepped through the front door.

The silence that answered him sent a cold rivulet of worry through him. Had something happened? He suddenly realized he hadn't seen her car.

She'd seemed fine when he'd left. Had she started having pains? Had the morning sickness returned with a frightening vengeance?

He raced from the living room into the kitchen and instantly saw the note on the table. His fingers trembled as he picked it up and read:

Chance,
   I can't stay. We had an agreement and I think it's best if we stick to it. You never intended to be a father and you're free to go back to the life you led before our crazy bargain.
   Thanks for two of the best months of my life.
                                        Lana

He read the note twice, as if somehow the words might change in the second reading. But they didn't.

He set the note on the table and went into their bedroom.

The closet door hung open and it was apparent that most of her clothes were gone. She was gone. The dresser top once again held only his things, none of hers. The only item left behind was the candle on her nightstand, its vanilla scent a haunting reminder of their nights spent in mindless passion.

He sank down on the edge of the bed, his head whirling. She'd released him. She'd released him to go back to the life he'd led before her, but the problem was he didn't want to be released.

He couldn't imagine going back to his solitary lifestyle. He didn't want a succession of unfamiliar women, didn't want an endless chain of impersonal motel rooms and strange towns.

When he had made the decision to remain here and be a husband to Lana and a father to their children, it had never entered his mind that she might not want the same thing.

How arrogant he'd been to assume that she might want him in her life. How egotistical to just take for granted that she'd want to remain married to him, might want to build a real and lasting marriage with him.

All she ever wanted was a sperm donor. Sarge's words from one of Chance's nightmares came back to haunt him. You aren't a keeper, boy.

"Stop it," he murmured aloud, halting the familiar old hurtful refrains. He was finished listening and believing his father's words.

He was not a loser.

He was not worthless.

But at the moment he felt utterly lost.

Lana. His heart cried out her name. How was she going to manage raising two children alone? Why wouldn't she want him to help her, to support her?

He left the bedroom, unable to stand the haunting scent of the candle any longer. He returned to the kitchen and read the note yet again.

Thanks for two of the best months of my life. He read that particular line over and over again. Confused, he set the note aside and slumped down at the table.

If the last two months with him had been the best in her life, then why wasn't she here with him now? Why would she want to end what they'd been building? And why...why would she want to deny those babies their father?

He needed to talk to her. He needed to make her understand that she needed him, that those babies needed him. He couldn't just let her run from him. He had to run after her.

Thankfully, on the day of their wedding ceremony, he'd picked her up at her apartment, so he knew that was probably where she would be now.

Adrenaline pumped through him as he raced to his car and pulled away from the ranch. He felt frantic, as if he were about to fight for his life. It was an unpleasant feeling, one he'd never experienced before.

He released a sigh of relief as he pulled up before

her apartment complex and saw her car parked in one of the spaces out front. Good, she was here.

He bounded up the stairs to her second-floor apartment and knocked rapidly on the door.

There was no reply.

"Lana," he called through the door as he knocked once again. "Please open the door. We need to talk."

Still there was no reply. He tried the door, but it was locked. "Lana, please. This is important. You can't just leave me like this. We need to talk about it. You need me...the babies need me."

The door to the next apartment opened and a wizened old woman peered out at him. Chance frowned in frustration. "Do you mind? This is private."

The old woman snorted. "It isn't too private with you yelling through the door loud enough for half the town to hear you." She slammed her door with a snort of indignation.

Still Lana's door remained closed and no sound drifted out from within. Maybe she wasn't here, after all. Perhaps Maya had picked her up. A wave of overwhelming despair swept through him.

Reluctantly, Chance left the apartment and got back into his car. He had to find Lana, but he didn't know where to look. All he really knew was that he didn't want to return to the ranch without her. She belonged there...with him.

Meredith sat in the back of the patrol car, one hand clutching Emily's. Rand sat in the front seat with Detective Thad Law, and another patrol car followed behind theirs.

Nobody spoke and Meredith's attention was focused intently on the scenery that flashed by outside the car window. Home. She was finally going home.

Rand turned around and offered her a supportive smile. Her heart expanded with love for the handsome son who had worked so hard to make it possible for her to reclaim her place as a Colton.

Meredith knew when Rand had initially contacted the authorities in Prosperino with the outlandish story of twin sisters and Patsy's deception, they had all been reluctant to accept his wild claims.

Thankfully, Rand had a sterling reputation and a stubborn streak a mile long. He'd talked and talked and finally somebody listened. Meredith showing up at the police station that morning had stunned everyone who knew Patsy as Meredith Colton.

Meredith refocused her attention out the window, a surge of excitement coursing through her as she recognized familiar territory. Within minutes she saw the terra-cotta roof rising in the distance and her heart leapt. Home.

She remembered! The impressive columns, the covered porches, everything was suddenly achingly familiar. She felt tears burning behind her eyelids as overwhelming emotion swept through her.

Emily pulled at her hand, making Meredith realize she'd been squeezing it too tightly. She released her hold and flashed Emily a smile. "Sorry," she whispered.

Emily nodded, but didn't return Meredith's smile. Meredith ached as she saw the deep shadows of misery that clung inside Emily's beautiful blue eyes.

Had Emily suffered a cut, Meredith would have applied antiseptic spray and a Band-Aid. Had she been burned, Meredith would have smoothed on soothing aloe vera and covered the wound with a clean bandage. But Meredith had no idea how to ease the soul sickness inside Emily. She had no idea how to fix the young woman's broken, spiritless heart.

As Meredith once again gazed out at the house, her heart pumped an unsteady rhythm. Almost home. Within moments they would be parked before the big elegant home and the past would meet the present. Within moments she would know if she truly had a loving, caring husband or if she'd idealized him in her dreams and fantasies.

The patrol cars turned into the circular driveway and the tension inside Meredith peaked so high she wanted to scream. It had been the vision of strong arms around her, holding her close, that had kept her going through these lost, lonely years. It had been dreams of a large hand holding hers, of a solid body pulling her close, that had made her fight to reclaim her past.

Had those dreams and visions been of Joe? Why, oh why, couldn't she remember his face? Why, if their love had been so good, so strong, had her mind erased his features from her memory?

The cars parked in front of the house and Rand turned around in the seat to face her. ''It's going to be all right, Mom.'' His handsome face shone with fierce determination. ''You wait here. Let me and the detective talk to Patsy first.''

Meredith nodded and watched as Rand, Thad Law

and two officers approached the front door. Once again Emily reached for Meredith's hand, as if needing the lifeline only a mother could offer.

"It's going to be all right now," Meredith said to Emily. "Nobody is ever going to try to hurt you again." A fierce love welled up inside her, first for the child Emily had been, a child who had tried to tell everyone something wasn't right with her "mother," and for the woman she'd become, who had three times faced a killer because she refused to believe that Patsy was Meredith.

Meredith wrapped her arms around Emily and kissed her forehead. "Everything is all right now, Emily."

Emily's eyes welled up with tears. "Then why do I feel like nothing is ever going to be right again for my entire life?"

Meredith's heart cried for Emily's pain. She stroked her hair, kissed her forehead again, then released her and stared at the house, where Rand and the officers were at the front door.

Meredith's breath caught in her throat as Patsy stepped out the front door. Even though she'd known Patsy had usurped her identity, had stolen her life, seeing her twin sister step out her front door was like being slapped soundly across the face.

Dressed in a beige Chanel pantsuit with a colorful scarf at her neck, Patsy looked every inch the lady of the manor.

Although the two women were identical twins, there were now subtle differences between the two. Patsy's hair was slightly longer and blonder than Meredith's, showing the effects of expensive salon care. Even from the distance that separated the two, Meredith could see the bloodred polish of Patsy's long nails, so unlike Meredith's short, unpolished ones.

Myriad emotions raced through Meredith. Anger, swift and self-righteous, was tempered with pity for the troubled sister who would resort to such horrific measures.

"Would somebody please tell me what is going on here?" Patsy's strident voice rose in the air.

Meredith opened the car door and stepped out, her gaze focused on the sister who had betrayed her so completely. "Patsy," she called softly.

Patsy turned her head and her eyes widened as she saw Meredith. The flare of her eyes was there only a moment, then gone. "Oh, you found her. You found Patsy!" she exclaimed.

"It's over, Patsy," Meredith said as she approached her twin sister. "It's over. I remember everything. I remember the car accident that you caused so you could steal my life. How could you do something like this? How could you?"

A high-pitched burst of laughter escaped Patsy and she gazed first at Thad, then at the officers. "Poor dear. She's always had mental problems. Did you know she spent time in prison?" Patsy's voice held just the slightest tremor of nerves.

Meredith heard a car door slam and realized Emily must be approaching them. Patsy's gaze swept past Meredith to the young woman.

"Emily! Darling, I've been so worried about you," Patsy exclaimed.

"You tried to have me killed," Emily cried as she came to stand next to Meredith. "You sent that awful man after me and he killed Toby."

"Emily, you're overwrought and not making sense. Why on earth would I want to have you killed?" Patsy's voice was soft and on the surface sounded full of love. But Meredith heard the underlying tension.

"You want me dead because I know the truth," Emily exclaimed as tears coursed down her cheeks. "You want me dead because I know you aren't my mother." She grabbed Meredith's arm. "This is my mother. This is the real Meredith."

Again Patsy looked at Thad and the officers, her eyes holding a tinge of panic. "Gentlemen, I really don't understand what's going on here, but this woman is my sister, Patsy Portman. She suffers from mental illness and she has obviously twisted poor Emily's fragile brain."

"Cut the crap," Rand said roughly. He looked at Thad. "I want her arrested."

At that moment Joe stepped out the front door, a bewildered frown on his face. "What's going on?" His gaze fell on Meredith and he froze.

In that instant of eye contact, the floodgates of Meredith's mind opened, releasing memory after memory of love. And in that instant, Meredith knew why her mind had refused up until now to release those precious memories of her husband.

"Joe...my Joe," Meredith said softly as tears filled her eyes.

Patsy grabbed Joe's arm possessively. "Joe, tell them. Tell them I'm Meredith. Tell them I'm your wife.'' Her voice was a full octave higher as she clutched at Joe. ''Make them all go away. I demand you make them leave.''

Joe didn't seem to hear her. His gaze remained locked with Meredith's and he shrugged off Patsy's grasping, clutching grip and took a step toward Meredith. ''Meredith?''

His strong, familiar voice sent a shiver of sweet heat through her. ''It's me, Joe. It's me.'' Before she got the words entirely out of her mouth, he was reaching for her and wrapping his arms around her.

''I demand you take this woman away,'' Patsy shrieked. ''*I'm* Meredith Colton. That woman doesn't belong here! Arrest her! Get her out of here.''

''You don't belong here,'' Rand replied and nodded his head to the officers.

Patsy screamed a protest as the policemen moved toward her. ''You're making a mistake,'' she screeched as they cuffed her hands behind her back. ''I'll have your jobs for this. I'll see to it you never work again. *I'm* Meredith Colton. That woman is an imposter. I'm Meredith Colton and this is my home.''

Patsy was still screaming threats and warnings as they stuffed her into a patrol car and drove off. Still Joe held tight to Meredith as if he were afraid she'd somehow slip away from him.

And she reveled in his tight grasp, smelling the achingly familiar scent of him, celebrating the warmth of his body against hers.

''Come on, Emily,'' Rand said and wrapped his arm around his sister. Together they went into the house, leaving Meredith and Joe alone.

Joe cupped Meredith's face in his hands, his blue eyes filled with wonder. "It is you, isn't it?" he said softly. "I can see in your eyes that you're my wife...my beloved Meredith."

"Oh, Joe, I've missed you so." Tears once again blurred Meredith's vision as she gazed at the man she loved, the man whose aura had given her strength over the past ten years.

"I thought I'd lost you forever." His blue eyes darkened and his features twisted into a tortured grimace. "I couldn't understand how you could become a woman I hated. I couldn't understand how we'd gotten so lost to each other. I should have known she wasn't you. I should have known!"

"Shh," Meredith placed a finger on his lips. "How could you know? I never told you about Patsy. You had no way of knowing I had a troubled twin sister who could do such a thing. I was wrong...so wrong."

This time he placed a finger over her lips to halt her words of self-recrimination. "My sweet Meredith," he whispered.

"My sweet Joe," she returned. Eagerly their lips found each other's in a kiss of explosive joy, of rediscovery and of enduring love.

When the kiss ended, Joe took her gently by the arm. "Come inside, love. We have so much to talk about, so much to catch up on."

"Yes, I want to go inside." She squeezed his arm, her eyes once again filling with tears of joy as her heart expanded with love. "Oh, Joe, it's so good to be home."

Fourteen

Lana awoke the next morning exhausted and ill. She remained in bed waiting for the morning sickness to pass and tried not to think of Chance. But not thinking of him was as difficult as not drawing her next breath.

He had remained outside her apartment for most of the afternoon and evening. She'd heard his confrontation with her neighbor then had heard him leave. But he'd returned soon after and begun the barrage anew. Occasionally he'd knock on the door and call her name, his familiar voice aching in her heart. But she'd remained steadfastly silent, refusing to give him any indication that she was even home.

It was close to midnight when he finally gave up and she'd watched him pull out of the apartment parking lot. She'd wanted to run after him, tell him she would spend the rest of her life with him, that perhaps she loved him enough for the both of them.

But she knew they'd both regret it. He would eventually regret being bound to a woman he didn't love, to a ranch that had never been home and to babies he'd never counted on. She would watch him grow more and more unhappy and she would regret her own decision to keep him bound to her through a loveless marriage.

She rolled over in her small, single bed, her body aching for Chance's arms around her, his chest beneath her fingertips, his legs entwined with hers. She remained that way until almost noon, then with her morning sickness waning, she got up to face a lonely day.

The items she'd brought from Chance's house had not been unpacked, and as the coffee brewed, she eyed the suitcases with dread. Unpacking was the final step in reclaiming her life alone, but she wasn't ready to face it yet.

Instead she curled up on the sofa with a cup of coffee and wondered what Chance was doing at that very moment. Did he miss her just a little bit, or had the relief of being set free already seeped through him?

He'd probably put the ranch back on the market already, itching to go back to the Midwest and start his own business.

And she would remain here and have her babies. His babies. She looked around the small apartment. Eventually she'd have to move. This apartment was rented for a single woman and was far too small for a woman and two children.

Tears filled her eyes and her heart ached from loving Chance. In two months he'd captured her heart entirely. She felt as if by leaving him she'd deprived herself of a basic essential of life. But she absolutely couldn't stay with him, knowing he was staying only for the sake of their babies.

She drank two cups of coffee before she realized it was Halloween and she didn't have a piece of candy in the place. She knew from years past that the apartments always got lots of trick-or-treaters.

Within an hour she'd dressed and got in her car to head to the store for treats. The discount store was filled with frantic mothers and crabby kids shopping for last-minute costume needs.

"But I wanted to be a skeleton," a little boy about seven wailed.

"There aren't any skeleton costumes," his mother replied. "Look, you can be Dracula instead."

"I don't wanna be Dracula. I want to be a skeleton," the little boy protested.

The mother looked at Lana and rolled her eyes, then gazed again at her son. "If you're Dracula, we can get fake blood and put it on your face."

The little boy's face lit up. "Fake blood? Cool!"

Lana left the two and hurried to the candy display. Someday she would be that mother, good-naturedly arguing with two children over Halloween costumes.

But before they got old enough to understand about Halloween, there would be diapers to change, midnight feedings and fussy times. Trying to handle two babies alone would be exhausting.

At least she knew she could depend on her mother and her sister to help when necessary. It wasn't as if she were all alone, even though without Chance she felt all alone.

She paid for three bags of candy treats, then headed back to the apartment. There was no sign of Chance's car in the parking lot, and when she got inside, there were no messages on her answering machine.

He'd given up. The relief she knew he'd eventually feel apparently had already grabbed him. It was over. Truly and irrevocably over.

When she got back inside her apartment, she began to unpack, and as she unpacked, she wept. Because her babies would not have a father. Because she would never have Chance.

Chance sat in the kitchen, listening to the silence of the house around him. Lana had been absent from the house before, but never had the sound of her absence resonated so loudly.

Before he'd been fully awake that morning, he'd reached for her, and had come away with empty arms and an aching heart.

Work, he'd thought. Work was the panacea for whatever ailed you and with that thought in mind, he'd gotten out of bed, dressed and spent the morning repairing the Sheetrock in the spare room.

The baby store had promised delivery of the cribs

by noon and sure enough at fifteen minutes before twelve, the delivery truck had arrived.

Chance had spent the next two hours moving furniture out of the room and putting together the two cribs. When he was finished, he stood in the doorway of the room and stared at the beautiful baby beds with their lacy canopies.

The room was perfect for babies. The eastern window allowed in the morning sun and the floor space easily accommodated the two cribs.

If he closed his eyes, he could easily imagine the sounds of babies cooing, of a rocking chair creaking, and of Lana singing sweet lullabies. And at that moment he came to a decision.

He didn't want the ranch, not if Lana wasn't here. And she wouldn't live here as long as he was here. Lana loved this place. Her love and caring was evident in every room of the house.

She'd placed her mark on it with flower arrangements and pictures on the walls, with shiny wood and spotless floors. She belonged here far more than he did. His babies belonged here.

Lana didn't want to spend her life with him. Right from the beginning she'd made it clear she didn't intend for him to be a father to her children. But he didn't want his children raised in a series of small apartments, without room to play, without room to grow.

They belonged here. More than he ever had. This ranch would be his legacy of love to his babies, to Lana. But before he deeded the ranch to her, he wanted to talk to her, needed to make sure there was positively no room in her life for him.

With this thought in mind, he showered and dressed, then headed away from the ranch and toward the Colton house. It was the only place he knew of that Lana might be.

Perhaps she'd parked her car at her apartment complex just to throw him off the trail and she was really staying with her mother and father. If nothing else, Inez would know where her daughter was.

Inez herself opened the back door in answer to his knock. "Oh, Chance, have you heard the news yet?" Her dark eyes shone and her cheeks were pinkened with excitement.

"What news?" Chance asked as she grabbed his arm and pulled him into the kitchen.

"It's nothing short of a miracle," Inez exclaimed. For a moment Chance wondered if she was talking about Lana carrying twins. But before he could say anything, she continued. "Who knew that Meredith had a twin sister? Who knew that our poor sweet Meredith was suffering amnesia and living in Mississippi while her hateful twin was living here, pretending to be her?"

Chance's head whirled as Inez filled him in on the drama that had taken place the day before. "I haven't seen Joe this happy for ten years," she said, tears of joy sparkling in her eyes. "The two of them are sitting in the courtyard now, like two lovebirds. We finally have our family back together."

Family together. The words echoed with pain in

Chance's heart. That was what he wanted. He wanted his family all together. "Inez...where's Lana?" he asked.

She frowned. "Chance, I don't want to get involved in your business with Lana. I didn't approve of this whole thing from the very beginning."

"You don't have to get involved, just please tell me where she is." He heard the desperation in his voice, and apparently she heard it, too.

"She called me last night from her apartment."

"But I was at her apartment all evening and nobody answered my knocking." A wave of grief swept through him as he realized that Lana had been there all along, but had refused to open the door to him, had refused to even speak to him.

"She doesn't want to talk to you, Chance. She loves you so much. She loves you enough to let you go. If you can't love her like she loves you, then let her go."

Stunned by Inez's words, Chance nodded, murmured a goodbye and left the house. Surely Inez was wrong, he told himself as he drove toward Lana's apartment. Surely she was talking about the fact that Lana had once loved him when they'd been young. If Lana loved him now, then why had she left him?

She loves you enough to let you go. Inez's words reverberated around and around in his head. And she was letting him go because that was what she believed he'd wanted. Hell, it was what he'd believed he'd wanted until this very moment.

Now he knew. He knew the truth. He wasn't staying in Prosperino for the babies. He was staying because he was in love with Lana. He pressed on the gas pedal, knowing the only thing he had left to do was to convince her that he was a keeper.

Meredith sat next to Joe on the stone bench in the courtyard. They had spent most of the night talking, catching up on their years apart. Then they'd made sweet, wonderful love, restoring what had been stolen from them, renewing the commitment they'd made to each other so long ago.

Meredith looked around her, strangely at peace despite the fact that the gardens that had once been her pride and joy had gone to seed and lacked the vibrant flowers she'd always adored.

"This place was the one memory that survived the car accident and my amnesia," she said, breaking the peaceful silence that had lingered between them. She looked at the fountain, with its soothing gurgle and splash of water. "I dreamed of this place over and over again, and it upset me that I didn't know where it was or how to get back here."

Joe put his arm around her and pulled her close against his side. "And did you dream of me?" Joe asked.

She leaned into his familiar warmth, a sense of peace cascading through her. "I dreamed of a special man. I could feel his warm embrace, remember the touch of his hand. I dreamed of standing right here in front of this fountain and him placing a ring on my finger. The dream always brought me a sense of peace and also left me frustrated.''

''Frustrated?''

She nodded. ''Because I couldn't see the man's face.'' She turned in his arms so she could see his face now. ''No matter how hard I tried, I couldn't see your features…couldn't remember what you looked like.''

She saw the whisper of pain that shadowed Joe's beautiful eyes. She raised a hand and caressed his hair. On the day of the accident, his hair had been rich and dark; now the darkness was shot through with strands of silver. She thought him more handsome now than ever.

''I know now why I had absolutely no memories of you, why my mind refused to give me a glimpse of your face.''

''Why?'' he asked.

She placed her palms on either side of his handsome, distinguished face. ''Because remembering you would have been so painful, I don't think I would have survived. Because of all the memories that flittered through my mind over the last ten years, the memory of our love would have shattered me.''

He wrapped her in his arms and lowered his lips to hers. His kiss was passionate, yet gentle and filled with a wealth of love. When the kiss ended, Meredith once again snuggled against his body, her gaze scanning around the courtyard.

''I have a lot of work to do here,'' she said, remembering the way the courtyard had once looked.

"We need new flowers planted and all these weeds pulled."

Joe smiled. "We have the rest of our lives to plant flowers and pull weeds. And I have a feeling you will have more help than you need."

She smiled. "You're talking about the children." She thought of them all...her beloved family. Later she would spend time with them all, but at the moment she was content to spend these quiet moments with Joe.

Meredith sighed, her thoughts turning to her sister. "What's going to happen to Patsy?" she asked softly.

He hesitated before replying. "I don't know," he finally said. "We'll have to wait and see what the authorities decide to do. She's facing a number of charges."

"She needs help."

"Meredith, how like you to be worried about her after all she's done to you, to your family."

"I hate what she did, but I can't forget that she's my sister, my own flesh and blood." She sighed, and shoved thoughts of Patsy from her mind. "Joe, I'm worried about Emily. She's hurting so badly."

He nodded and took her hand in his. "I know. But hopefully time and love will heal her."

Time and love. Meredith smiled at her husband, her Joe. Yes, they had time and love, time to heal all wounds, and enough love to last them for the rest of their lives. "I love you, Joe," she said softly.

"And I love you." Once again he wrapped his

arms around her, his warmth suffusing her as his lips found hers.

Home, Meredith thought. Yes, she was truly home. Home in Joe's arms where she belonged.

Fifteen

It was the longest day in Lana's life.

With every hour that passed without a word from Chance, the knowledge that he didn't love her echoed in her weeping heart.

She had finished unpacking and had no tears left unshed, so she took a nap. When she awakened, she felt more in control of her emotions.

She took a long hot shower, then pulled her hair back in a tight bun at the nape of her neck. Chance loved her hair loose and flowing. She would never again wear it that way.

As dusk began to paint the sky, she ate a light supper, then poured the candy she'd bought in a large bowl and set it by the front door in anticipation of the trick-or-treaters.

At least the evening would pass quickly with the little costumed munchkins at the door, she thought. Perhaps it would pass so quickly she wouldn't have time to entertain one single thought of Chance.

As she ate, she thought of her conversation with her mother the night before. Inez had been brimming with the news about Meredith Colton's return. "She and Joe are acting just like newlyweds," Inez had proclaimed after she'd explained the whole situation to Lana.

Lana had been thrilled with the news. Joe and Meredith had once shared a relationship that had been the envy of half the town. They'd worn their love for each other on their faces.

The news also brought with it a bittersweet pang in Lana's heart as she wished she and Chance had somehow managed to find the same kind of relationship.

Within an hour the parade of fairy princesses, cowboys, bewhiskered kittens and devils began. Lana had always enjoyed Halloween, but this Halloween seemed even more special as she thought of the babies she carried inside her.

The babies. That was what she had to focus on. Although she didn't have and never would have Chance in her life, at least she'd have his children to love and to raise.

"Trick or treat," a boyish voice yelled through her door.

She opened the door to see a youthful pirate complete with eye patch and hook hand.

"It's really a trick," the boy said, then stepped aside. Chance suddenly filled the doorway.

"Go away," Lana said at the same time her eyes drank in the sight of him. He looked so achingly handsome in a pair of charcoal-gray dress slacks and a long-sleeved striped shirt.

"I'm not going away until we talk," he replied as he stepped over the threshold and closed the door behind him.

"We have nothing to discuss. Our deal is over, our bargain is fulfilled." She looked away from him, afraid that if she looked into his eyes, gazed at his beloved face, she'd acquiesce to whatever he wanted.

"Lana—" He broke off at the series of knocks on her door.

"Trick or treat. Trick or treat," a chorus cried.

Chance stepped out of the way as Lana opened the door. She quickly gave each child their treat, then once again closed the door and turned to face Chance.

"Please, Chance. Go home. Sell your ranch and follow your dreams."

"Sometimes dreams change." He frowned in obvious frustration as another knock sounded on her door.

Lana once again took care of the trick-or-treaters.

"Come to the ranch with me, Lana. We can talk without interruption there." He reached out and placed a hand on her shoulder.

She stepped away from him, finding his touch painful. "I told you, we have nothing to talk about."

He raked a hand through his hair and his eyes were

stormy seas of turmoil. "Thirty minutes, Lana. All I want is thirty minutes of your time. But it has to be at the ranch. Please." The word was a mere whisper and his face held a naked vulnerability she'd never seen before.

"Okay," she heard herself say and instantly wanted to call the word back.

A moment later they were in Chance's car, both silent as they drove toward the ranch.

Lana wanted to kick herself for agreeing to this madness. She'd said her goodbye, to the ranch and to him. What could possibly be gained by thirty minutes spent with the man—and at the ranch she'd wanted to call home?

"I would have never opened the door if I'd known you were there," she said, breaking the silence.

"I know that. It cost me ten bucks to get the kid to knock on your door, then disappear. He drove a hard bargain."

A hard bargain. No, the real hard bargain had been the one she and Chance had made. The bargain that had, on the surface, appeared to be an answer to both their dilemmas.

They didn't speak another word until Chance pulled up in front of the house. "I'm here, so talk," she said, not moving from the car.

"Don't be difficult," he chided. "Come inside and we'll talk over coffee."

She didn't want to go inside. She didn't want to step into the place where she'd been so happy. She didn't want to smell the familiar scent of Chance ev-

erywhere, remember the moments they'd spent together.

"Thirty minutes," she reminded him as she reluctantly got out of the car. "And then you take me right
back to my apartment."

"It's a deal," he replied.

She followed him into the house, but paused as he
headed down the hallway. He turned and looked at
her, his expression unreadable. "I want to show you
something in the spare room," he said in explanation.

Curious despite her hesitation, she continued to follow him. When they reached the doorway to the spare
room, he opened it up and she gasped in surprise.

The cribs. The beautiful cribs she'd seen in the
store. Someplace in the back of her mind, she also
registered that the wall had been fixed.

"They belong here, Lana," he spoke softly from
just behind her. "And you belong here."

She turned to him, tears of pain, tears of anger
welling up in her eyes. "Why are you doing this to
me?" She struck out at his chest with her fists. "Why
are you making this so hard?"

She shoved past him and down the hallway, needing to escape the scene of the beautiful cribs her
babies would never sleep in.

He caught up with her in the living room and
grabbed her by the shoulders to stop her from running
out the front door. "I can't let you go, Lana."

"You have to let me go," she cried. "We agreed.
We made a bargain."

"So, sue me for breaking it," he exclaimed, his

voice thick with frustration. "Sue me for changing my dreams, for realizing how empty my life was before you. Sue me for wanting to be a father to my children. But for God's sakes just don't cut me out of your life!" He dropped his hands from her shoulders. "I can't figure out how this got so screwed up."

Lana knew how things had gotten so screwed up. She'd fallen in love, and despite the fact that she was carrying Chance's babies, she would not, could not sacrifice herself to a man who didn't love her back. She sank down on the sofa. "I don't know, Chance. When I first proposed this whole thing, it seemed incredibly simple. You get what you want, I get what I want, then we both walk away."

He sat down next to her on the sofa and expelled a deep, long sigh. "Lana, I want you here. I want my children to be raised here, where they'll have room to grow and play. If you won't stay here with me, then I'll deed the ranch over to you and the children and you can live here without me."

She looked at him in shock. "You can't do that," she protested. "The whole reason for us getting married in the first place was so that you'd have this ranch. Sell it, Chance. If you don't sell it and use the money to start your own business, then what will you do?"

He shrugged. "I can always continue to sell tractors and combines."

"But that's not what you wanted," she protested.

"Lana, I don't want to sell the ranch. I want you to have it." He broke their eye contact and stared down at the top of the coffee table. "If all my dreams came true, then we'll all live here together. You, me and our children. But I don't know how to make that happen. I don't know how to tell you how much I need you."

"What?" Her heart seemed to stop beating in her chest at his unexpected words.

He looked back at her, his eyes tortured pools of emotion. "I need you, Lana." The words seemed to seep out of him reluctantly. "I need you in my life. I love you, Lana."

Once again tears sprang to her eyes. "You're confused. You mean you love the babies. They are the reasons you want me in your life. They are the reasons you want the marriage to continue."

"That's not true, Lana." He took her hands in his, holding tight so she couldn't pull away. "You want to know the truth? When you told me you thought you might be pregnant, I was disappointed. I wasn't ready to give you up."

His words stole her breath away, but still she was wary. "Chance, I don't want you to stay with me and then grow resentful and angry. I couldn't bear if I thought that I had ruined your life."

"Lana, the only way you can ruin my life is if you leave me." His eyes shimmered luminously, like green mists in the moonlight. "I love you, Lana, and it's you I want to spend my life with. I want to grow old with you, and watch our children and our grandchildren grow. I want you in my bed every night and sharing all my days with me."

"Chance Reilly, if you don't kiss me this very moment, I think I just might die," Lana gasped.

He didn't disappoint her. His mouth captured hers in a kiss that was a combination of hunger and love. Lana responded with all the passion that burned inside her for him, all the love she'd tried so hard to deny.

"I love you, Lana. You're everything good in my life," he said when the kiss ended.

"Oh, Chance, how I love you," she said as she swiped at the happy tears that filled her eyes. "I loved you when I was thirteen and I still love you with every ounce of my being, every beat of my heart."

He gathered her against his side and pulled the pins from her bun, releasing her hair from its confines. "I was afraid to love you, afraid that somehow I wouldn't be the man you needed in your life."

Lana opened her mouth to protest, but he placed a finger against her lips, then continued. "All my life, my old man told me I was worthless, not good for anybody. I wasn't a keeper. And for most of my life, I believed him."

His eyes radiated love as he gazed at her. "But somehow you managed to dig out the poison of those old feelings. You made me realize who I really am, what I'm really capable of, and what I want from life. And what I want is you."

Lana's heart filled with the glory of his words, the wonder of his love. She placed a hand on his cheek and gazed into his gorgeous eyes. "You are a keeper, Chance Reilly. And I intend to keep you for the rest of my life."

Again his mouth claimed hers and in it was the hope for their future, the joy of their desire, and the dreams on which they'd build a marriage for years to come.

This time when he broke the kiss, his eyes shone with a distinctly heated glitter. "You know it's Halloween night," he said. "And if you come into the master bedroom with me, I think I might just be able to arrange a treat."

She smiled. "Are you sure this isn't another trick?"

He laughed and stood, then pulled her up into his arms. "You can tell me later."

As he carried her down the hallway, Lana wrapped her arms around his neck. Her thoughts drifted to Meredith and Joe, together again after all the years. Lana felt as if it had taken years for her to gain her heart's desire. She'd fallen in love with Chance years ago and had dreamed of being his bride.

It had been a young girl's love and a young girl's fantasy. But the love that blossomed in her heart for him now was that of a mature woman. She knew that they would fill this house with children and laughter, and most of all love.

*Don't miss the continuation
of* THE COLTONS
with Kasey Michaels's
THE HOPECHEST BRIDE.
Look for it in June 2002.

One

Josh Atkins shifted his body slightly in the saddle and looked across the distance, toward the outbuildings, the red tile roof of the Hacienda de Alegria.

Must be nice, living in a place like this. Safe, protected. Money coming out your ears.

Money to buy safety, to buy silence. Money enough to sweep all the nastiness under a hand-braided rug and forget about it, go on your merry way, get on with your life. Laugh, dance, sing. Eat good food, sleep in a warm bed.

While Toby lay in his cold grave. Forgotten in his cold grave.

Josh tipped back his Stetson, exposing his thick, unruly brown hair, the piercing blue eyes that squinted toward the rapidly setting sun. His skin was deeply tanned, with sharp lines around his eyes from a lifetime spent squinting into that sun, riding the range in between stints on the rodeo circuit. Slashing lines bracketed his mouth, grown deeper, harder, since the news had come to him about Toby just as he was up for a big ride in Denver.

Josh's body was whipcord lean, taut and solid muscle. Taller than Toby, older than Toby by four years, definitely less handsome than Toby, whose boyish good looks had mirrored a pure and caring soul.

There was nothing pure or caring or good in Josh's soul as he glared toward the Hacienda de Alegria. There was only hate, a deep and abiding hatred he'd fed with newspaper articles about the grand and glorious Coltons, a hate he nurtured every time he looked at photographs of his brother…his laughing, loving brother who had died because Emily Colton had tricked him into thinking she loved him.

That's how Josh saw it, and he had reason to believe he was right. He had the letters Toby had sent him, letters full of the beautiful Emma Logan, how much Toby admired her, loved her, damn near worshipped her.

Emma Logan. Emily Colton. One and the same woman, the woman who had come to Keyhole, Wyoming, hiding her identity, hiding her reasons for being there.

Josh remembered Toby's first mention of Emma Logan, how he had checked her out in his capacity as sheriff, because her physical description had closely matched that of a female connected to a car theft ring operating in Keyhole. How Toby had berated himself in the letter that had followed, explaining to his brother that he'd been wrong about Emma, that the beautiful young woman had come to town to try to forget losing her fiancé in a traffic accident, to try to rebuild her life.

Toby had thought he was just the man to help her do exactly that, and Josh had laughed over his brother's letters after that, as Toby had told him of his visits to Emma's cottage, the mega-cups of coffee he drank at the local café where she worked, just so he could be near her. He spoke of her sweet and dimpled smile, her thick mane of long, chestnut-red hair, the graceful way she moved, the softness of her large blue eyes.

Toby had fallen, fallen hard.

And all that time, Emma Logan had been lying to Toby. Emily Colton had been *using* Toby. Using him so that she'd feel safe, knowing that she'd come to Keyhole, not to get on with her life, but to hide from whomever it was she believed was trying to kill her. All of that, and more, Josh had learned from Toby's enraged fellow officers in Keyhole when he'd come to bury his brother.

If she'd told Toby, alerted him to the danger, then maybe Toby would still be alive.

But she hadn't told him, and Toby had died not knowing why, and probably still believing Emma Logan might have one day loved him. He'd died, alone on the cold floor of her cottage, and she hadn't even stuck around to explain. She'd just left him there as he lay bleeding to death, and she'd run, run back to her cushy family and her money and her life.

Bitch. Cold, heartless, conniving bitch.

Josh pulled on the reins, turning his mount, heading back the way he'd come, back to the nearby ranch where he'd taken a temporary job, just so that he could be near the Hacienda de Alegria, just so he could be near Emily Colton. One day meet Emily Colton. One day tell Emily Colton exactly what he thought of her.

Then maybe he could finally learn to deal with his own guilt.

magazine

quizzes

Is he the one? What kind of lover are you? Visit the **Quizzes** area to find out!

recipes for romance

Get scrumptious meal ideas with our **Recipes for Romance.**

romantic movies

Peek at the **Romantic Movies** area to find Top 10 Flicks about First Love, ten Supersexy Movies, and more.

royal romance

Get the latest scoop on your favorite royals in **Royal Romance.**

games

Check out the **Games** pages to find a ton of interactive romantic fun!

romantic travel

In need of a romantic rendezvous? Visit the **Romantic Travel** section for articles and guides.

lovescopes

Are you two compatible? Click your way to the **Lovescopes** area to find out now!

Silhouette®

where love comes alive—online...

SINTMAG

Every day is

A Mother's Day

in this heartwarming anthology
celebrating motherhood and romance!

Featuring the classic story "Nobody's Child" by Emilie Richards
He had come to a child's rescue, and now Officer Farrell Riley was
suddenly sharing parenthood with beautiful Gemma Hancock.
But would their ready-made family last forever?

Plus two brand-new romances:

"Baby on the Way" by Marie Ferrarella
Single and pregnant, Madeline Reed found the perfect husband in the
handsome cop who helped bring her infant son into the world. But did his
dutiful role in the surprise delivery make J. T. Walker a daddy?

"A Daddy for Her Daughters" by Elizabeth Bevarly
When confronted with spirited Naomi Carmichael and her brood of girls,
bachelor Sloan Sullivan realized he had a lot to learn about women!
Especially if he hoped to win this sexy single mom's heart…

Available this April from Silhouette Books!

Visit Silhouette at www.eHarlequin.com   PSAMD

MONTANA *Bred*

From the bestselling series

MONTANA MAVERICKS

Wed in Whitehorn

Two more tales that capture living and loving
beneath the Big Sky.

JUST PRETENDING by Myrna Mackenzie

FBI Agent David Hannon's plans for a quiet vacation
were overturned by a murder investigation—and by
officer Gretchen Neal!

STORMING WHITEHORN by Christine Scott

Native American Storm Hunter's return to Whitehorn
sent tremors through the town—and shock waves of
desire through Jasmine Kincaid Monroe....

Silhouette®

Where love comes alive™

**Silhouette Books presents a dazzling keepsake
collection featuring two full-length novels by
international bestselling author**

DIANA PALMER

Brides To Be

(On sale May 2002)

THE AUSTRALIAN
*Will rugged outback rancher Jonathan Sterling
be roped into marriage?*

HEART OF ICE
*Close proximity sparks a breathtaking attraction between a
feisty young woman and a hardheaded bachelor!*

You'll be swept off your feet by Diana Palmer's BRIDES TO BE.

Don't miss out on this special two-in-one volume, available soon.

*Available only from Silhouette Books
at your favorite retail outlet.*

Coming in May 2002

**Three Bravo men marry for convenience—
but will they love in leisure? Find out in
Christine Rimmer's *Bravo Family Ties!***

Cash—for stealing a young woman's innocence, and to
give their baby a name, in *The Nine-Month Marriage*

Nate—for the sake of a codicil in his beloved
grandfather's will, in *Marriage by Necessity*

Zach—for the unlucky-in-love rancher's chance to
have a marriage—even of convenience—
with the woman he *really* loves!

BRAVO
FAMILY TIES

Silhouette®
Where love comes alive™

Visit Silhouette at www.eHarlequin.com   BR3BFT

These New York Times *bestselling authors
have created stories to capture the hearts and minds
of women everywhere.
Here are three classic tales about the power of love—
and the wonder of discovering the place
where you belong....*

FINDING HOME

DUNCAN'S BRIDE
by
LINDA HOWARD

CHAIN LIGHTNING
by
ELIZABETH LOWELL

POPCORN AND KISSES
by
KASEY MICHAELS

*Available only from Silhouette
at your favorite retail outlet.*

Where love comes alive™

Visit Silhouette at www.eHarlequin.com   PSFH